ADAM

7 Brides for 7 Soldiers
Book 2

ROXANNE
ST. CLAIRE

Adam
7 Brides for 7 Soldiers

Copyright © 2016 South Street Publishing
Print ISBN: 978-0-9970627-7-9

Published in the United States of America

Critical Reviews of
Roxanne St. Claire Novels

"St. Claire, as always, brings a scorching tear-up-the-sheets romance combined with a great story: dealing with real issues starring memorable characters in vivid scenes."
— *Romantic Times Magazine*

"Non-stop action, sweet and sexy romance, lively characters, and a celebration of family and forgiveness."
— *Publishers Weekly*

"Plenty of heat, humor, and heart!"
— *USA Today's Happy Ever After blog*

"It's safe to say I will try any novel with St. Claire's name on it."
— *www.smartbitchestrashybooks.com*

"The writing was perfectly on point as always and the pace of the story was flawless. But be forewarned that you will laugh, cry, and sigh with happiness. I sure did."
— *www.harlequinjunkies.com*

"The Barefoot Bay series is an all-around knockout, soul-satisfying read. Roxanne St. Claire writes with warmth and heart and the community she's built at Barefoot Bay is one I want to visit again and again."
— *Mariah Stewart, New York Times bestselling author*

"This book stayed with me long after I put it down."
— *All About Romance*

7 Brides for 7 Soldiers

*Meet all seven sexy seven soldiers
of Eagle's Ridge, Washington!*

Dedication

Sometimes neighbors are the people who live next door, and sometimes they are the friends you rely on through thick and thin. This book is dedicated to Cyndi Stowe and Chris Rodenhurst who not only helped hook up our generator so I could finish writing this book after a hurricane hit, they are also former U.S. Coast Guard officers who made sure I had my facts straight for a Coastie hero. Thank you for all the love, laughter, and wine we've shared as neighbors and friends.

ADAM

Chapter One

Adam Tucker peered into the shadows of a drafty, dingy, far-from-finished former boathouse and huffed out a breath of pure frustration. He had three weeks, but he needed three *months* for this Herculean task.

Damn his brother and his wild ass and endless bets. And damn that last shot of Jack Daniel's for making him take a Zane Tucker wager. After sharing thirty-two years on earth and nine months in the womb, Adam should know better than to bet his twin.

But finishing the transformation of a boathouse into a camp dorm had seemed like a no-lose proposition at Baldie's last night. The hardest part of the construction work was done, and Adam already had interest from YMCAs and youth programs all over the Pacific Northwest to book adventure tours for kids later this summer. He *could* finish this remodel in three weeks, even if Zane used words like *impossible* and *in over your head* and *furniture shopping*.

Holy hell, he hated to shop for a pair of jeans, let alone everything he'd need to finish this project. Beds, chairs, dressers, sofas. And appliances. And...*shit*. He still had to install the cabinets and build stairs. And probably paint the entire place. Nah. A bunch of kids wouldn't care if there was a little gunboat-metal-gray primer on the walls, right?

His gaze traveled up to the second-floor loft and the bank of windows that ran under the rafters on three of the walls. Windows that had been shuttered for years since his grandfather abandoned this place long before Adam was even born.

Kids wouldn't care if it was dark, either. Hell, they were just going to sleep in here.

He had only three weeks until spring weather ushered hundreds of tourists into Eagle's Ridge, and they'd descend upon A To Z Watersports to rent kayaks, paddleboards, and canoes, or take white water rafting trips down the Snake River. Adam and Zane would be slammed with business, even if they did hire another guide or two. There'd be no time for Adam's "side" project.

Speaking of hiring, wasn't someone supposed to be here for an interview? He checked his watch and noted the prospective employee was ten minutes late already. Good river guides were hard to find, so he wouldn't hold it against her, but he'd have to cut the interview short now. Well, he'd just throw her into a raft so she could show him her stuff and he could get back to this job. There was still so much left to do to make this old building a place to rescue kids who needed it the most.

Still, he'd better see if the interviewee was in the rental office waiting for him. He crossed the wide wooden planks he'd refinished himself, appreciating the shine and almost-invisible nails, one of the many things he was proud of in this building.

When he'd come home to Eagle's Ridge from his last Coast Guard station two years ago, he'd had the idea to turn this place into a living quarters for a youth camp right away, buying the deserted boathouse for a song from his grandpa Max.

The structure had been abandoned for years, situated on the far side of prime riverfront property Adam's grandfather had claimed back in the forties when Eagle's Ridge had first been founded. Grandpa built a big old house, which was now A To Z headquarters on the first floor and Adam's apartment on the second, and erected the boathouse to rent out space to local canoers and kayakers. That business fizzled over the years, and the building slipped into disrepair, used for little more than storage.

But Adam was changing all that.

And if just one teenager got high on nature instead of drugs, then he would have had succeeded. At least, maybe he'd succeed in wiping out a little of the endless supply of guilt that he'd carried since the day he left Kodiak, Alaska. One failed rescue shouldn't have wrecked him or his career, but it had.

Now, he knew what he had to do, and if his brother said it had to be finished in three weeks or wait six months?

Then he'd do it in three weeks, damn it.

He yanked open the heavy wooden door and walked smack into sunshine. And woman.

They both jolted backward at the unexpected contact.

"Oh, oh, sorry." She blinked up at him, but his eyes were still adjusting to the sunlight. "Are you Adam Tucker?"

Then his eyes cleared so he could get a better look. A much better look. "You're..." *Gorgeous.* "Here for the interview?"

Surprise widened ebony-dark eyes and sent long,

black lashes up to perfectly arched brows. She wore makeup for an interview that she knew included a trip down the river? That was a first.

"Wow, you guys are quick around here," she muttered.

Late and sarcastic, too? She better know her way around some rapids.

His hand still on the door, he closed it behind him, not willing to waste interview time answering questions about his pet project.

"We try." But the only thing he was *trying* to do was not stare. Impossible. She was so...so...so *not* a watersports guide.

"River rats" had a look he'd come to know and expect. They all had sun-washed, freckled skin with that faint smell of the rapids clinging to wash-and-wear hair. The dudes were rugged and fearless, the chicks were natural and sunny. Female guides were built for watersports with strong upper bodies, flat chests, and muscular thighs from hundreds of hikes and miles of swimming.

This woman looked like the only swimming she did was poolside in a bikini. She smelled more like flowers than the river, and those tumbling layers of black hair had clearly been in the hands of a professional. If she'd seen the sun, it was from under a hat and a thick layer of SPF 50, because her skin looked like pure whipped cream. And her body wasn't flat, muscular, or built for anything but...yeah, that.

Definitely built for that.

"You're ready to interview?" he asked, knowing he had an edge of challenge in his voice, but honestly, he'd already made his decision. This babe was *not* seaworthy.

"Of course," she said. "That's why I stopped in at the front desk at..." She gave a vague gesture in the general direction of the business. "A To Z Watersports, is it?"

She couldn't even bother to know the company name before showing up? Strike…five, hot stuff.

"That's what we call it." Let her figure out that A and Z referred to owners *Adam* and *Zane* Tucker.

"Well, I was asking about a job, and they sent me…" She glanced behind him at the former boathouse, those pretty brows drawn in an expression of confusion. "Here."

"Same business," he said. "Just a different department. I'm Adam Tucker." He reached out a hand and noticed that she hesitated just a moment before shaking it. With red-painted nails, no less.

"I'm…" She cleared her throat and nodded once. "Jadyn McAllister."

Even her name was too glam for a guide. "Jadyn," he repeated, letting the pretty sound settle on his tongue.

"Like the stone, with an n. Jade-en."

He realized that he still held her hand, which was soft and tender and…had never gripped an oar in its life. "Been out on the Snake River much?"

"No. I'm from Miami."

"Miami?" He covered his laugh with a cough. "Like Miami, Florida?"

"That would be it."

"They have watersports down there?"

"Water? In Miami? You do realize Florida is surrounded by water on three sides?"

Really, the last thing he needed to hire was a smartass who had to blow-dry her hair before taking out a rafting tour. "Miami just seems so different from here."

"It is," she agreed. "But I'm a fast study, a hard worker, and I'm looking for work. I was told you have a job that would be perfect for me."

There was the most imperceptible note of desperation

in her voice that twisted something in his gut. "Well, I need to hire someone and fast, but…"

He let his gaze drop over her, taking in the way a white sweater clung to her curves and accentuated that veil of gleaming hair the color of a midnight sky. A thin, cotton sweater with no jacket in forty-five degrees. That probably explained why she had both arms wrapped tightly, denying him a full look and making him think about giving her his down vest.

She wore jeans so tight he could see every line of her long, lean thighs, finished off by high-heeled black boots peeking out from under the denim.

Heels. *Seriously*. On a watersports guide?

"Are you sure you can do this?" he asked.

She just lifted a brow.

"No offense," he said quickly, kicking himself for talking without thinking. Now she was going to throw some labor law at him for saying something politically incorrect or insulting in an interview. Zane was so much better at this than he was.

"None taken," she assured him. "It's just that you don't even know my qualifications yet."

"True. Résumé?" He held out his hand.

"Oh, I left it over there. The man behind the counter read it and sent me straight here, telling me I should just talk to you."

The man behind the counter. Of course Zane would think it would be hilarious to send a beauty contestant over to distract Adam from winning the bet. "Let me guess. He looked just like me."

She frowned. "He had darker hair, but…yeah." She considered him for a moment, her gaze moving up and down his body just slowly enough to make him uncomfortable. "He was bigger."

Bigger? He snorted. "Yeah? You should have seen him as a kid. Went from scrawny to brawny, and his idea of a joke is as massive as his chest, that's for sure. Sorry, but you're not what I'm looking for."

Her jaw loosened. "Based on…what?"

On the obvious fact that she was no river rat. But, fine. He'd play the game. He held up his hands in surrender. "You're right. I'm being an ass."

"Ya think?" she mumbled, turning to hide the comment, but he caught it, loud and clear.

"Let's just get going so I can see what you got." He nodded toward her jeans and boots. "You bring your own gear and clothes?"

"My clothes are fine. My gear is between my ears. Why don't you start by telling me what it *is* you're looking for?"

"What I'm looking for is someone with enough experience to know you can't wear high-heeled boots and skintight jeans," he shot back.

She blinked at him. "What would you have me wear, Mr. Tucker?"

"How about a wet suit, booties, and a splash top that says you're not afraid of getting good and soaked, if that is indeed even true?"

She stared at him for a second, then her eyes shuttered closed. "You know what? I don't need a job that bad." She backed away. "It was a stupid idea. And that other guy seemed *really nice*."

As opposed to what Adam was being, but come on. He needed a river guide, not a runway model. "Because my brother's trying to derail me and distract me," he explained.

She frowned. "That's not what he said, but honestly? I'd rather starve." She pivoted and started

7

across the lot, in the direction of Sentinel Bridge.

That's right, princess. Go to the better side of town where you belong.

Every single step tortured him with a back view that was as fine as the front. He stared until she walked along the wide section of the bridge and hesitated at the door to No Man's Land, the restaurant his dad owned. The whole time, Adam had one thought echoing in his brain: Zane really needed to die.

"Oh my God, I'm so sorry to be late!"

Adam turned to see a woman powering toward him, a huge smile and a smattering of freckles over suntanned skin.

"I'm Holly Dillard, certified seaworthy kayak and rafting guide." She held out a hand and shook Adam's with a no-nonsense grip and a palm full of paddle calluses. "You probably don't remember, but we met last summer on the Salmon River, where I've been a guide for thirteen years."

He let go of her hand, still processing her introduction as he glanced down at the wet suit she had on under a loose water jacket. "You're…the guide interview."

"It's been a dream to live in Eagle's Ridge and work for A To Z Watersports. What do you say we take a kayak out and let me show you how I roll?" She flashed a warm smile that lit her whole face and made her eyes twinkle. All without a spec of makeup. Or sarcasm.

"Okay," he said slowly. "Let's go get the boats."

On the way to the dock and put-in, she chattered about the rapids rise and last month's floods and when she worked a summer at the Columbia River Gorge and…Adam glanced over his shoulder.

If this was his guide interview, who the hell was that other woman?

"Pick a vessel," he said, indicating a row of kayaks roped along the docks. "I'll be right back. I need to talk to my brother for a second."

He took the back door into A To Z Watersports, walking through the kitchen break room, where Gambler, Zane's yellow lab, snoozed contentedly on his dog bed in the corner. That meant Zane was here for sure because that crazy ass dog went wherever his master went.

He strode over ancient scuffed wood and inhaling the morning scents of coffee and doughnuts someone brought in. He passed the two offices that were once a bedroom and dining room, into the old-time parlor that now served as the business reception area. There, Zane was at the desk, finishing up a call.

"So?" His brother tapped the cell phone to disconnect and looked expectantly at him. "Do you owe me a beer or what?"

"A beer?" Adam stared at him, long used to the fact that his twin brother was a near-carbon copy, except Zane had dark brown hair and Adam's was bleached light by the sun. Yes, Zane was bigger, thanks to his gym time, but they had the same jaw, only Adam's was clenched right now. Same smile, not that Adam was wearing one at the moment. And the same eyes that straddled blue and green, depending on the color of the sky and their moods.

Right now, Adam's mood was surprisingly foul.

"You think I'm so dumb I'm going to take Miss Miami Heat out on a kayak and lose my whole day of work? You really want to win this bet that bad, Bro?"

Zane's dark brows drew together. "It's just a bet, Adam. Anyway, it's more fun if I give you an unfair advantage and still win."

"How in the hell does she give me an unfair advantage? The only thing she gave me was a headache." And an ache a little lower, but he'd jump naked into a freezing river before he admitted that to his brother.

Zane looked more perplexed, then glanced at the desk in front of him. Picking up a sheet of paper, he held it out for Adam. "I saw this résumé and thought she'd be exactly what you need."

"If I needed..." His gaze dropped to the words on the page under the name Jadyn McAllister.

Professional interior decorator...residential and commercial...contractor's assistant...equipment and furnishing...design assistant. Winner of the Markham Space Planning Award for interior design.

Adam just closed his eyes.

"I thought she could help you, man, but if you're determined to do this on your own, you better be prepared to lose. And the loser has to—"

"I know what the loser has to do." Adam slammed the paper back on the desk. "Can you take Holly Dillard on a guide test?"

"I have a better idea." Zane gave a wry smile. "Why don't you just hire Holly and then go find the unfair advantage you just gave up?"

Adam hated to admit it, but that was a damn good idea.

Chapter Two

"Hot coffee?"

Jane looked up at the waitress who'd handed her the menu, meeting soft green eyes and a warm smile. She stared for a moment, not quite focused because the white flashes of fury behind her eyes hadn't yet subsided.

"You okay, hon?"

Hon. Well, that beat *Jadyn*, which still didn't quite roll off her lips yet. No lie ever had been easy for Jane McAllen, and now she was forced to tell a whopper every time someone asked her name.

Use the name Jadyn McAllister. It sounds familiar, but not your own name. Never use any other name, especially not your real one.

At the echo of the warning, a fresh wave of dread rolled through her. Well, at least Adam "You're Not What I'm Looking For" Tucker had made Jane forget her predicament for ten minutes.

"What I need is a good stiff drink," she replied.

"No booze here, sweetheart, but plenty of comfort." The woman's eyes sparked with a sweet, maternal warmth as she flipped a long dark braid over her shoulder to reveal a name tag that said Brenda. "I can break a lot of rules and coerce the cook to make some creative menu substitutions, but the one thing you can't do at No Man's Land is drink. Made that rule thirty-five years ago when this place moved to neutral ground. No drinking, no fighting. Course, they go hand in hand. You want that, head to Baldie's. You can get some mean cheese fries, but they're not open for breakfast." She grinned. "So what can I get you, hon?"

Other than cash and a phone call that said the coast was clear? Not much. "Coffee for now."

Brenda pulled out an old-school order pad and flipped a few pages, but she was still studying Jane closely. "Cream and sugar?"

"I guess." Jane exhaled slowly as the last of the adrenaline that had spiked settled in her system, then she looked up at Brenda. "Is there anything worse than a man who assumes he knows everything about you and misjudges you instantly?"

The waitress considered that, squishing a face that had probably passed fifty, but was attractive and approachable. "An *ugly* man who assumes he knows everything about you?"

That made Jane smile and remember Adam Tucker's unexpected mix of sun-dappled hair and mountain-rugged features, and those haunting aquamarine eyes that coasted up and down her body as if he didn't quite believe what he saw.

"Well, he isn't ugly, that's for sure. A condescending, assumption-making douche canoe, but he is hot as hell and built like a Greek god."

Brenda gave a knowing nod. "There's a few like that around here, but that's the curse of being a military town. Lots of high-quality testosterone on the banks of this river, but that means the place is crawling with alpha men who can be as irritating as they are gorgeous."

"So I discovered." She flipped the menu open, then closed it again. "What do you recommend?"

"For someone with the blues? As much sugar and carbs as we can fit on a plate."

"I like the way you think, Brenda."

She started writing. "Get the HALO pancakes topped with snow and drowned in rocket fuel."

Jane blinked at her. "Excuse me?"

"HALO—high-altitude low opening. It's a stack of six cakes. Snow is whipped cream, and rocket fuel is Sam's homemade maple syrup that'll give you energy on the battlefield of life." She recited the speech as if she said it two hundred times a day.

"HALO," Jane repeated. "Another curse of the military town? Menu items named by the Pentagon?"

Brenda laughed. "You're catchin' on, sweetheart."

Jane had done very little research when she'd chosen Eagle's Ridge, Washington, as her temporary hiding place. Her "relocation planning" had been done for her when an FBI agent named Lydia Swann had escorted her to Miami International and shoved a ticket to Seattle, along with her own driver's license, into Jane's hand. Lydia had promised that they looked enough alike that she'd sail through security with it.

And she had.

Lydia had also given Jane a couple thousand dollars in cash and a phone she shouldn't use to call anyone in Miami, but was to never let out of her sight in case it rang with the news that she could come home. Oh, and some final instructions: *Don't leave Washington but get as far off the grid as you can and trust no one until you hear from the FBI telling you it's safe to return.*

In Seattle, she got on a bus headed west to Walla

Walla, but that was bigger than she'd expected, so she used the fake license to rent a car and drove to a place called Eagle's Ridge, as far into the mountains and the southeast corner of the state as she could go.

She'd been there for a week and was running out of patience and money.

"So, is there a base nearby? Is that what you mean by a military town?"

"Oh, no, not a military base," Brenda said. "It's our history. And, I guess, our present."

Brenda angled her head toward the row of windows that looked out over the river to the other side of town, all of it nestled in the shadows of a snowcapped mountain range. "Can't go ten feet without bumping into someone who has served, is serving, or is planning to enlist. But that's what the old coots had in mind when they staked their claim on Eagle's Ridge back in 1945— a legacy of military men and women."

Despite the woman's world-weary tone, Jane could hear a note of pride in her voice.

"That's interesting," Jane said. "I've never heard of a town like that."

"We are definitely unique."

"I assume non-military folks are welcome, too?" Jane asked.

"Of course. Hikers, rafters, newcomers, passersby. Which one are you?"

"I'm going to…spend the summer here." With luck, she'd be gone long before the summer ended, but she didn't add that.

"Really." Brenda eyed her with far more interest now, looking her up and down a little like Adam Tucker had, only without the curled lip. "Our tourist activities don't usually attract someone so…" She searched for a word just long enough for Jane to brace for a little more judgment from the locals. "So *sophisticated*."

She gave a dry laugh. "You'd think I'm the first person who's ever worn heels and makeup in this town."

"Not at all, but we do attract the earthier types. What brings you here, hon?" she asked with open curiosity.

Jane managed a casual shrug, because the only honest response to that question was: *If I told you, you'd never believe me.*

Less than ten days since it happened and Jane still wasn't exactly sure how she'd gone from having a perfectly normal life as an interior designer for Miami Beach's wealthiest residents…to a woman in hiding for her life.

"Oh, you know, the usual reasons a thirty-year-old picks up and starts over in a brand-new place," Jane said.

"A man?" Brenda guessed.

"Yup." A *man* would do nicely as her reason for running. It wasn't a lie, really.

Sergio Valverde was a man. A man who apparently controlled one of the largest drug trafficking rings between South America and Miami. A man who wrongly believed that Jane was no interior designer, but a mole who'd attempted to turn him in. A man making wrong—and evidently deadly—assumptions about her, because Jane hadn't even known her client was a drug lord. She'd thought he was just a stupidly rich Bolivian with questionable taste in art.

"So what's your line of work?" the waitress asked.

"I'm an interior designer," Jane said. The FBI agent told her to keep her story as close to the truth as she could, so she wouldn't get tripped up. "And if you know of any work around here, I'd be interested."

She preferred to do the work she loved, which was why she had been excited when the nice man at the watersports company told her that they *might* have something in her field. And then she walked right smack into Adam Tucker.

So it was back to plan B.

From her handbag, she pulled out the local paper she'd purchased and pointed to the paltry Help Wanted section that had gotten her to the watersports company in the first place. They'd just advertised an "opening," which had been enough to entice her to make a résumé at a local office supply store. Of course, it had no real references and displayed her new, made-up name since Lydia warned her not to use the driver's license except to rent a car. Other than that, she was not to use it.

Oh God. She was so not cut out for this. And what happened, anyway? She got judged. Wrongly.

"There's always jobs around here during the season," Brenda said sweetly. "We just filled a slot, but there are lots of little restaurants and stores in town, just across this bridge."

"I've been in town," she said. "And I do need something since I'm living in a..." Seedy motel. "Hotel." On cash, which could easily run out if the FBI took too long to keep their end of the bargain and put Sergio Valverde in jail.

"Are you staying at the Broadleaf?" Brenda asked, checking her out again and nodding as if she not-so-secretly believed that Jane looked like she belonged at that posh place in the middle of town.

"Uh, no." She managed a weak smile. "The Hideaway Hotel." Really, how could she resist with that name and seventy-nine-dollars-a-night rooms?

The Hideaway *did* earn her a curled lip. "Yeah, they

have a lot of nerve calling that a hotel. So, yes on the HALOs?"

Jane puffed out a breath. "If they're not priced by the Pentagon, too."

The other woman laughed. "I'll put an order in, dear. You relax and enjoy the view. Pretty sure you're not getting one like this at the Hideaway."

When Brenda left, Jane dropped back in the chair and let her gaze skim the restaurant décor, which was probably not the view the kindly waitress had meant.

Yes, the mountains were majestic, and the river was about a thousand shades of navy and gray with a few dramatic whitecaps in the wide expanse between here and the section of town on the other side. But Jane was an interior designer, and her interest would always be, well, the interior.

The beamed ceilings and local landscape paintings on the walls gave the place a real and rustic vibe that relaxed her as much as the comforting smell of fresh coffee and buttery biscuits.

Truth was, she'd been tense since the day she'd opened her door to greet Lydia Swann, a woman she knew only as the "friend" of one of Jane's largest and most demanding clients. Her stomach still tightened when she relived the moment she'd looked at Lydia's FBI badge and tried to follow the words spilling out of the woman's mouth at lightning speed.

Only some of them had actually made sense at the time.

Sergio Valverde is an international drug trafficker... The FBI is closing in and nearly had him... Your life is in danger... We'll get you out safely... Stay away...

Jane still couldn't believe the Bolivian billionaire who'd hired her to redecorate his Miami Beach penthouse was a wanted drug kingpin. Okay, maybe she could believe that. He was loaded beyond description and pretty darn shady.

But then to learn that Lydia Swann wasn't one of the many "hangers-on" in Sergio's massive entourage, but an undercover FBI agent who'd infiltrated the operation and almost brought Sergio in on a sting that went south? Mind-blowing.

Not as mind-blowing, however, as the news that Sergio had been told a woman had turned him in and he firmly believed that Jane was the rat.

And apparently, Bolivian drug lords *killed* rats.

She lifted a thick ceramic mug, took a deep drink of coffee, and choked on it when Adam Tucker barreled through the front door. Speaking of rats.

"Hey, Brenda." He marched to the counter, and half the heads in the place turned to watch. The female half.

But Jane's blood boiled for a completely different reason. Who cared if a man stood at least six feet and filled out a T-shirt with mouthwatering muscles? Yes, his jaw was square, his eyes were piercing, and he probably had dimples if he ever smiled. But, hello?

You're not what I'm looking for.

He leaned over the counter and called for the waitress again, who had her back to him pouring coffee. She merely held up one finger to tell him to wait, but he tapped the counter with palpable impatience.

He turned left and right, glancing down the long counter, then around the restaurant, scanning the place like a man looking for...*her*.

His haunting, stunning, impossible-to-ignore blue-green gaze landed right on Jane, and his strong shoulders fell a bit. In relief? Hard to say, because he blinded her with a smile so gorgeous, she forgot to check for the dimples.

A smile? Was he freaking serious? Before she could take her next breath, he called over his shoulder. "Never mind, Brenda. I found her."

What?

She stared at him as he strode across the restaurant, threading the tables with ease, pinning her with an expression she couldn't even begin to read. Without a word, he pulled out the chair across from her, sat down, and looked directly into her eyes.

"I screwed up."

Not what she was expecting. "You don't say."

He flinched. "You're mad."

All she did was raise a brow.

"I had no idea, none whatsoever, that you were an interior designer. I thought you were interviewing for a job as a river guide, and so, obviously, I...you...guides are..." He searched her face, no doubt looking for help. "Lifeline, please. This man is drowning."

She lifted a shoulder, trying to ignore just how damn good-looking he was when he wasn't condescending, but it was impossible.

"You want me to drown," he finally said.

"And there you go assuming you know what I'm thinking again."

He dropped back in the chair and puffed out a breath. "Could we try again? Start over?"

"Or we could start right at the part where you say, 'You're not what I'm looking for.'"

He flinched like she'd hit the target. "Again, I thought you were a white water rafting and kayak tour guide. Am I right in assuming you've never even been in either of those vessels?"

Of course he was, but she didn't want to give him the satisfaction of being right about anything. "Vessels?

Who calls a kayak a vessel?"

"A former Coastie." He tipped his head at her frown. "A rescue swimmer with the US Coast Guard."

Ah, of course. One of the many military men Brenda told her about. "I admit," she said slowly, "I've not done a lot of, uh, kayaking." Fact was, she couldn't swim and would probably just as soon drop over Niagara Falls as get into white water for fun.

A half smile curled his lips. Oh damn. Yes to the dimples. "So I was not completely off base."

"Oh, you were off base," she assured him.

"And in my defense, you didn't tell me that you were a decorator."

"Designer."

"A *decorated* designer, I mean, based on your very impressive résumé."

"Are you sucking up to me, Mr. Tucker?"

"Like you wouldn't believe." He leaned closer and moved his hand like he wanted to touch hers, but thought better of it. "I need your help."

"Remodeling your condo on the water?"

He raised a brow. "If that's what you want to call a one-bedroom on the second floor of A To Z, but no, that's not what I need. This isn't about me."

But something told her with a guy like Adam Tucker, it would always be about him.

"I've seen your résumé." He inched closer, holding her gaze with the confidence of a man who knew that look got him whatever he asked for. "And I'm here to swear to you that you, Jadyn McAllister, are exactly what I need."

For a long moment, she held his gaze, hating that the exchange made her a little bit dizzy. The way he said her fake name made it sound kind of pretty and alluring, so much so she almost wanted to get a little closer and hear him say it over and over again.

But that would be against the scant list of rules Lydia had fired off as she helped Jane throw clothes in a suitcase—because that frenzy couldn't be called *packing*—for a trip she had never expected to make.

Make up a simple story and stick with it. Lie low, don't make friends. And, for the love of God, do not trust anyone.

But what if her money ran out?

"Oh, is this your douche canoe?" Brenda set a pile of pancakes in front of her with a thud on the table.

Adam's jaw unhinged. "Your…*what*?"

Jane smiled, nodding thanks to the waitress, who looked from one to the other with a wry smile before walking away.

"What's a douche canoe?" he asked.

She tsked and shook her head, picking up her fork as she eyed the over-the-top pancake stack. "Why, it's a vessel, of course."

As she slipped her fork into a puffy cloud of cream, he reached over the table to stop her from taking the bite. "Will you help me?"

"No."

He choked softly. "You don't even know what I want."

Oh, she knew what he wanted. And in any other place or time or circumstance, she might consider giving it to him, because Adam Tucker was hot.

Even his fingertips singed her skin.

"Can I tell you and then you can make an educated decision?" he asked, undaunted.

"No." She slowly slid her hand away from his touch and lifted the whipped-cream-laden fork to her lips to slide it into her mouth. Swallowing, she gestured toward the stack. "I'd like to eat in peace."

He stared at her for a good, long ten seconds. Long enough for her to memorize every handsome feature. Long enough to shake up every dormant hormone. Long enough to make her hold her breath when he reached over the table and blithely ran a finger along her lower lip.

She managed not to react or break eye contact.

"You missed some," he said in a low whisper.

Without a word, he sucked the whipped cream off his finger, stood up, walked across the restaurant, and disappeared into the kitchen.

Jane didn't move except to flick her tongue over her lip, which was still searing from his touch.

Smart move turning that job down. He was nothing but trouble, and she had enough of that in her life.

Chapter Three

Dad wasn't nearly sympathetic enough as Adam relayed his dilemma. He listened, nodding, but Sam Tucker was in full work mode at the grill of a kitchen that hadn't seen a major update in several decades. Simple, clean, and low-tech, the kitchen that looked out toward the luncheon bar was a comforting place to Adam, considering he'd spent a decent amount of his childhood here.

The original restaurant, Max's Diner, owned by Grandpa, had been shuttered before Adam was born. When Dad took over the business some thirty-five years ago, he'd moved Max's to this unique location on the Sentinel Bridge in the shadow of the founders' statues that stood sentry at the bridge's entrance. The new location not only helped attract more business from the tonier east side of the river, it placed the restaurant on "safe" ground for those feuding founders who'd been memorialized in uniform by a sculptor.

Because of that, Max's Diner became nicknamed No Man's Land, and at some point, Dad had officially changed the name, and the landmark restaurant had thrived. Well, it thrived because of Dad's cooking, Adam remembered as he watched his father in action and sucked in a breath of sizzling bacon.

"Did you fix the Master Guns?" Brenda asked as she breezed into the kitchen.

"Just about done." Dad looked up from the grill, his face softening a little. "That customer didn't give you a hard time, did he?"

She waved off the question. "Nothing I can't handle, Sam."

"Is that all you wanted, Son?" he asked, distracted by the food again and maybe not 100 percent worried about Adam's problems with the boathouse conversion.

"Unless you have an answer for how I can get her to change her mind."

"Guess you could find another designer type to help you."

A little unexpected punch hit his stomach. He could, but...

"Don't think he wants another one," Brenda said with two raised brows. "Do ya?"

"Well, she's...convenient."

"And a jaw-dropper, too."

Adam managed a get-real look. "Brenda Morgan. How long have you known me?"

"I assume that's a rhetorical question," she replied. Of course it was. Brenda had been his mother's best friend, and she'd worked in his family's diner for as long as he could remember. She'd been there through the ugly days, when Mom had peeled out for fame and fortune, and had helped Dad run the business while their divorce was finalized. She'd stuck around all these years, too.

Through it all, she'd picked up the broken pieces of the Tucker kids, cleaned up the messes they'd made as teenagers, and handled the girlie stuff with Bailey when

Dad, Zane, and Adam were clueless about the lone female in the family.

"Then you know she is not my type. I can't stand all that makeup." Though he wouldn't mind smearing her lipstick or seeing what those red-tipped fingers could do.

"True," Brenda conceded. "She doesn't look like she'd hike up the mountain and sleep under the stars."

"Exactly." He snorted at the thought of Miss High Maintenance participating in what was his idea of a perfect Saturday night. "I want the boathouse transformation done, especially because I have a bet to win."

"Oh, that Zane." Dad shook his head, laughing. "Sure got the gambling gene from my dad."

"Harmless gambling," Brenda added, always ready to defend any of Sam's kids like they were her own.

"Well, I want to win the bet, but only because I want to finish the project even more. That woman can help me, so I need some advice on how to persuade her."

"I got nothin'," Dad said, his attention fully on some eggs on the griddle.

When Adam sighed in frustration, Brenda put a hand on his arm. "How about I give you a bit of useful intelligence?"

"Anything," Adam said, leaning both hands on the pass until Dad slid an order of eggs Benedict across the stainless steel.

"Here's your Master Guns with heaping extra camouflage," he said.

"Oooh, Sam. Look at that plate. It's absolutely gorgeous." She patted her apron. "Let me get a picture."

"Of the eggs?" Adam asked, frowning as Brenda rooted around her pocket, pulling out an order pad first.

"I just enrolled in a photography class at Ridgeview Community College," she said, finally producing a phone. "The syllabus says we have a week on food photography, so I want to practice. Can you hold that plate so the light shines on the bacon?"

Adam threw a glance at his father, expecting to see him looking just as perplexed, but he was looking at the griddle as he shook his head almost imperceptibly.

"Come on," she insisted. "Lift that side of the plate."

"Don't let those eggs slide," Dad warned with a slight edge in his voice.

He obeyed the order, lifting the plate of Master Guns.

"So, what did you find out about her?" he asked.

"Hang on." She snapped a few pictures, then turned the phone to get a different perspective.

"The eggs'll be as hard as grenades if you dawdle much longer, Bren."

She ignored Dad's warning and took a step closer and continued snapping shots. "She's running away from a guy who broke her heart," she said quietly.

"She is?" Adam almost dropped the plate.

"Yep. Living at the Hideaway and is so short on funds she's combing the newspaper want ads instead of her phone, like it's 1985 or something. Oh, and she eats sugar when she's stressed."

His eyes widened. "You got all that out of her in the time it took to order breakfast?"

She stuffed the phone back into her apron pocket and took the next plate as his father put it on the pass. "And she thinks you're hot as hell and built like a Greek god."

Dad chuckled from the other side of the pass.

"She does?" Adam asked, putting together this strange puzzle and getting no clear picture. "So if she needs a job, money, and wants a way out of a flea bag motel, why won't she even talk to this god who could be offering her all three?"

Brenda took a third plate of scrambled eggs and bacon—also known as two NCOs and train tracks—and balanced all three of them like a circus juggler. But she still managed to look at Adam with love in her eyes.

"I'll stall her check for you and you can try again," she offered on her way out.

Adam turned to his father, who was swiping a spatula over the grill when he looked up, his sky-blue eyes serious. "Sounds like you did jump to conclusions without checking the facts, Son."

"Yeah, you're probably right."

"So get out there and try it again." He added a wistful smile. "Sometimes that's hard with a woman, believe me."

He should know. Dad's efforts at dating had been pretty lackluster. But who could blame the guy after being unceremoniously dumped by a wife who chose to play a mom on television rather than be one in real life?

"I don't know, Dad. She shot me down pretty hard."

His father stood a little straighter, looking over the warming station to glare at his son. "How many tries, Son?"

"With her, just one, but—"

"With A-school?"

He frowned. Why was Dad bringing up AST training now?

"How many times did you try?"

Then he understood where Sam Tucker was taking this.

"Four," Adam replied, meeting his father's gaze with the same direct stare he'd have used on the chief petty officer who'd inflicted relentless physical punishment on Coasties trying to pass rescue-swimming school.

His dad nodded. "Four times until you got to be an

aviation survival technician." Dad always used the formal name for a Coast Guard rescue swimmer, and it always came out with tremendous pride. "You kept going back and going back, no matter how hard they made it for you."

"And I'd have tried ten times if that's what it took," he said softly. "Because that's what I wanted."

Dad angled his head. "So why are you standing here in the kitchen shootin' shit with your old man when what you want is in the dining room scarfing down my HALOs?"

Good question. Adam wasn't a quitter. But there was something about that woman. Something…unnerving. Something fake. Something—

Brenda came flying back in, an apologetic look on her face. "Couldn't do it," she said. "She didn't wait for her check, just put money on the table and left." She pointed toward the door. "Go get her while she's on a sugar high."

"Thanks, Brenda." Adam pushed off the counter and marched back into the dining room to catch a glimpse of dark hair outside the window, headed across the bridge toward town.

He shoved open the door and hustled to catch up with her, coming up behind her. "Excuse me, Jadyn? Miss McAllister?"

She didn't even slow down, and she had to have heard him.

"Jadyn!"

She stopped midstep without turning, but her shoulders sank as if she were just so completely over him.

When she didn't answer, he stayed a few feet behind her. "I'm redoing that boathouse over there, and I'm almost done with construction, but now I need some help with the, you know, design stuff. Buying furniture and finishings. The stuff that will take it from a big old warehouse to a nice place to live."

She still didn't answer. So he swung a little farther out on his virtual rope, throwing down a harness.

"I hate shopping," he said. "I can't actually think of anything I like less, to be honest. Like my teeth start to itch the minute I get into a store."

He heard an almost imperceptible huff of breath that might have been a laugh. Or a sigh of sheer disgust. But she still didn't turn to face him. Okay. Gotta reel this baby in.

"It's going to be a dorm for kids. At-risk kids. Kids without families. Kids in foster homes. Troubled kids. I'm trying to open a youth adventure camp for teenagers who might not have had a chance to go white water rafting or hiking."

He waited, let that sink in, and started to root around for just how far he had to go. Did he have to tell her about the one who—

"What do you know about those kids?" She spun around and asked the question so fast, he drew back in surprise.

"Enough," he answered, shifting his weight from one leg to the other. "Enough to want to give them something they can't otherwise have."

She narrowed her eyes, surprising him with the ice in her look. "You think they want a fancy vacation in the mountains?" Her voice rose. "Why don't you just write a check?"

"Because I don't want to. I'm not asking for your philanthropic guidance, miss, just…"

"Shopping," she finished.

He tipped his head in resignation while she stared hard at him. "There's more to it than that, but you are looking for a job, right? Starting over after a...a...bad relationship? Staying at the Hideaway?"

With each revealed fact, she inched back and her mouth opened a little.

"I've known Brenda forever. She's like a..." He swallowed, hating to admit that Brenda was more of a mother to him than his own mother was. "I trust her."

"And apparently, I shouldn't have," she said softly, inching away as she searched his face, then shook her head. "I don't think this is a good idea."

As she started to turn, he reached for her and she froze, staring down at his hand as it lightly gripped her forearm. Instantly, he let go.

"Good luck with your boathouse, Mr. Tucker."

He opened his mouth to argue, but even Adam Tucker knew when he'd been defeated. "Good luck with the job hunt, Miss McAllister."

Without a word, she turned and walked off, her long hair swinging, her shoulders squared, her pride—for whatever reason—completely intact.

Adam went back to the boathouse to get to work.

Chapter Four

Somebody outside in the parking lot was drunk. Jane pulled the scratchy blanket over her head and tried to block out the raised voices that could easily be heard through the paper-thin door of her Hideaway Hotel room. Then there was some laughter…quiet…and someone shouted a string of a few curses.

A car door slammed and tires squealed.

Oh God. How much longer would she have to live like this?

The question was so familiar to her, asked so many times, that frustration made her push the covers off and turn on the light. She blinked into the dinginess of her room, her gaze falling on a tear in the cheap grass cloth wallpaper, forcing herself to mentally renovate the room.

Completely reimagining her surroundings had been a coping mechanism Jane McAllen had invented when she'd been ten or eleven and had been moved to yet another of the "homes," as they called the places they shuffled kids with no families who had to be hidden from their parents. Not exactly fosters, not exactly orphans, but not exactly a member of any family anywhere. Kids who were biding their time until they were eighteen and no longer a burden on the county or child services or even the nice volunteers who brought hot meals at night.

As a young girl, Jane coped by looking at her room, wherever it was, and visualizing something beautiful. Bright colors, cheery curtains, lovely art. As she got older and found a stash of *Southern Living* magazines at a yard sale, her visions grew more elaborate. She'd put a wall here, add a window there, maybe include a pretty stone fireplace in her imaginary room.

Then she'd mentally decorate with a theme, finding one word or hearing a song that would reflect the mood she tried to create. She started to sketch, to dream, to realize ways to make ugly things and places and situations and people, even herself, more beautiful.

So what would she do with this place? First, she'd—

She startled at the soft hum of her phone on the nightstand. Finally!

"Yes, hello?" she asked breathlessly, pressing the device to her ear.

"It's Lydia."

She practically collapsed with relief. "Oh, thank God. I thought you'd never call. It's been a week, Lydia."

"And it's going to be a month, so sit tight."

"What?" she croaked. "A month? I can't stay here for a month!"

"Jane, listen to me, because I'm going to talk fast. I'm going to say this once, and you aren't going to hear from me again until Sergio is arrested."

"Okay," she whispered, clearing her head and trying to slow down the hammer of her heart.

"We are very close to getting this man, but a key piece of evidence has been lost. We are rebuilding the case, and it takes time. You cannot return, because he is 100 percent certain that not only are you responsible for his near arrest, but he thinks you have the evidence."

"That's crazy."

"Of course it is, but no one is going to defend you, because one of the people in the organization did take the evidence, and I need to find out who it is. It'll take us a few weeks, and then we will bring down one of the biggest drug rings on the East Coast."

Evidence. Organization. *Drug rings*. How did this get to be her life?

"You being gone is key to our success," Lydia continued. "So I've called to beg you not to come back. I know you want to."

"I'm running out of money," she said simply. "Could I go to a local FBI office and get help?"

"God, no. You're not officially in any kind of program," Lydia said. "My operation is completely under the radar. Just lie low for one more month. There are jobs that don't require a background check or Social Security number, Jane. Clean people's houses and get paid in cash. It'll tide you over."

She sighed, considering that, thinking of the few people she'd met who might help her. Brenda the waitress? The guy at the motel front desk? Adam Tucker?

"You're using the name I told you, right?"

She rolled her eyes. "Jadyn McAllister," she confirmed, hating even the sound of it. "But why can't I have used your name and license? It would help me get a job."

"It would help my cover get blown," she fired back. "Then we're all screwed."

Jane swallowed. "Okay."

Lydia sighed with what sounded like sympathy. "Look, I'm going to try and get some cash to you. Where are you staying?"

"The Hideaway Hotel in Eagle's Ridge, Washington." Jane slid her gaze over the dreadful room. "It's lovely," she added, layering in some sarcasm.

"I'll do my best to get someone to bring cash to you. What room?"

"Sixteen," she replied.

"Jane, listen to me," Lydia said in a low voice. "This is huge. This is serious. This man is responsible for moving drugs that kill people. People like you who've spent their entire lives trying to rise up from a bad situation."

Jane gasped a little. "How do you know anything about my situation?"

"I work for the FBI, Jane. I know that you were in and out of the Florida Child Protection program most of your childhood. I know who your clients are, your friends, and your entire online fingerprint."

"Why do you need to know that?" she asked, a low-grade panic rising. "Am I under investigation?"

"Anyone who came near Sergio Valverde was investigated by the FBI," she explained calmly. "And to put your mind at rest, I posted on your social media pages that you are on a much-needed extended vacation in the South Pacific. I even put up some pictures so your friends don't start filing missing-persons claims. We had someone call your other two clients and explain that you'd been called out of town."

The South Pacific? How the hell could they do that to a person? "This is ridiculous, Lydia."

"Dying is ridiculous, Jane. And if you step foot in Miami, that man will have you dead before you get through the airport. I am not kidding."

Her heart dropped so hard it was a miracle she didn't hear it hit the floor.

"We're doing this for your own protection, I promise."

Jane tried to swallow against a dry, tight throat. "I know."

"Now you just find a way to survive for a month, and this whole nightmare will be behind you. Make the best of it."

Make the best of it. How many times had some child-services professional said those words to her? A dozen? A hundred? Too many to count. And that's what she did her whole life. She made "the best" of it.

What was one more month? "Okay."

"Good girl. I'll call you when I have news."

On a sigh, Jane hung up and fell back on her pillows. In the distance, she heard a siren wailing, a sound she always found unnerving and frightening.

So she closed her eyes and tried to picture a room to redecorate and found herself wondering exactly what was inside an unfinished boathouse. She put herself to sleep imagining how she might decorate that.

The morning light peeked through the shutters of the boathouse, fighting and failing to brighten up the place. Sipping coffee after a restless night, Adam stared up the ladder that led to the loft, one more massive thing on his to-do list looming, literally, overhead.

He looked down at the inspection list left by the county manager a week ago and back up at the ladder. Without stairs that met code, he wouldn't get a certificate of occupancy. Without the CO, he couldn't open the door to anyone.

Forget the furniture and finishings and appliances, he wasn't done *building* this place yet. That's what he should be doing, while *someone else* was handling the interior design.

Okay, whatever. So he'd spent yesterday on a wild-goose chase just to have that wild goose bite him in the ass and saunter away. Fine. He had to get help from some friends.

And he had some really good ones, plus Zane. But his brother was up to his eyeballs getting the business ready for the season, and Ryder, who was damn near a real brother now, was busy expanding the airport he'd taken over.

But that wasn't all of the *magnificent seven*, as he used to think of the guys he had been in detention with for a whole semester of his senior year. They'd all gone off to different military branches, and some, not all, returned to Eagle's Ridge. But they stayed in touch, and they helped each other when it was needed.

Who should he call? Top choice for anything, not just construction, would be Wyatt Chandler, whom he considered one of his closest friends. But Wyatt was still serving as a SEAL, and Adam had no idea if and when he'd be back in Eagle's Ridge.

Jack Carter was a good man, but Jack made himself extremely scarce. Last Adam heard, he was supposed to meet up with Ryder for Founder's Day last month, but never showed, and no one had seen him in ages. Noah was in DC, or at least that's where Adam thought his last military assignment was.

Of course, as part of the family that owned Garrison Construction, his buddy Ford Garrison was an obvious choice, but he was currently back in Virginia. Ford had been in the construction battalion in the Navy, and that man would kill a set of stairs. They'd had a good long talk at Baldie's last month when Ford had been home for

Founder's Day, and Adam had even brought Ford to the boathouse to proudly show off his work so far.

Adam had taken plenty of shit for some of the corners he'd cut and a few mistakes he'd made, but Ford had given him some great advice, too. And he'd said to call if he needed help, so…

Saying the closest thing he knew to a prayer, he hit the button to call Ford.

"Hey, Adam. S'up?" The strong baritone was friendly and familiar, harking back to long Saturday afternoons when seven unlikely friends were forced together to play cards, make stupid bets, and ogle the hottest teacher at Eagle's Ridge High.

"What are the chances you're coming back home any time soon?" Adam asked.

"I don't know." He drew out the words, and Adam could picture those intense dark eyes as they concentrated on whatever problem Ford set out to solve. Give the dude a hammer, nail, and an engine part and he'd somehow manage to make it run, cut, mow, or fly. "Why would I go back to Smallsville and have to say hi to everyone in sight when I walk into No Man's Land?"

"Because I need stairs, man." He squinted up to the loft and did the roughest of rough estimates. "About fifteen of them."

"I knew the county inspector would nail you for that ladder."

"Yup. Nailed me like you're going to nail these stairs for me," he said hopefully. "Literally. With a hammer."

"Stairs aren't that hard, Adam. You need a few boards, a sander, and a basic understanding of geometry."

"Geometry?" Because something told Adam it was a little more complicated than that.

"Well, you have to take into consideration that the slightest discrepancy between steps can be a tripping hazard. You need to pay extra attention to that."

No, *Ford* needed to pay attention to that. Adam needed to go appliance shopping. He muttered a curse.

"I really need help," he admitted. "I have a ton of stuff to finish and three weeks before chaos hits the river."

"Tourist season. No, thank you. I don't want to be there then."

"We could do this in a weekend," Adam said. Then, after a beat, he added, "This weekend."

Ford groaned.

So Adam pulled out his trump card. "I bet Zane that I could do this in three weeks."

"Oh, in that case…" Ford said, laughing. Then his tone grew serious. "Dude, if my parents or my grandmother catch wind that I'm in town helping you build stuff, there's gonna be hell to pay. They've been all over me since I got out of the service about coming home and taking over Garrison Construction. It's not gonna happen, but they won't let it go."

"They'll have to get over that eventually, right?"

"You would think," Ford said with a weary sigh.

"So…are you saying you aren't up for this?"

Another pause and Adam found himself holding his breath.

"Is there any way a man could get in and out of that town and not be seen?" Ford asked.

Adam's brows drew together. Ford was a loner, no doubt about it, and he had some tensions with his family, but he really wouldn't want anyone to know if he was there? He didn't recall him hiding last time he was home.

"You could stay here, in the boathouse," Adam suggested. "That'd force me to get the beds. Bathroom's working, and anything you need would be at my apartment, right upstairs from A To Z, not two hundred feet away."

"All right, I can be there Friday," he finally said.

"Awesome, Ford. Really, thanks."

"I could use a little mountain air," Ford said, as if he didn't want to be accused too sharply of being the great guy Adam knew he was. "It's the people who drive me crazy in that town."

By *people*, he meant family. "Hey, I marked out a new trail if you're up for a hike after we finish the stairs."

"Stairs'll take a few days and a ton of work."

"I thought all you needed were some boards, nails, and basic math," Adam reminded him.

"Not *my* stairs," Ford said. "They'll be a freaking work of art."

Adam grinned, so grateful for this friend. "You want to fly into Spokane and take a puddle jumper to ER?"

"That'll work. I can be there Friday afternoon. And, man, do you owe me."

"So much."

When they hung up, Adam felt the closest thing to hopeful he'd felt since he'd walked in here this morning.

At least the stairs would get built this weekend. Now to measure for the beds, then the appliances.

"One step at a time," he reminded himself, grabbing the ladder rails to climb up to the loft. Now he *had* to have beds in here, so he'd better measure the space. As he reached the top rung and swung around the railing, the door opened downstairs with a soft squeak.

He mentally swore, knowing it had to be Zane

coming over to ask him to cover the desk or take out a tour. Which would be another two hours of his day gone.

"Uh, hello? Excuse me? Mr. Tucker?" The female voice floated up to the loft, a little soft, a little tentative, a little…familiar.

Slowly, without giving away his location, he inched forward to peer over the railing. Holy hell. It was her.

Jadyn McAllister turned, looking around with uncertainty, as if she expected him to jump out at her any second. He took the moment to study her, only a little surprised that she was every bit as attractive from above as in front or behind. Her hair was like black ink, thick and wavy and inviting. Her shoulders were narrow, but squared as if ready for a battle at all times. And her body had curves in the right places, but enough muscle to suggest she was tough inside and out.

Turning again, she pressed her knuckles to her mouth, a whimper that sounded like sheer desperation escaping from her throat and making him frown and lean a little closer. Maybe not *that* tough.

"Oh God," she murmured, a crack in her voice that felt like a knife going right through his gut. Still covering her mouth, she hissed in a breath. "Now I'm really in trouble."

She was?

Battling his inner need to swoop down and save a drowning victim versus the desire to listen and learn more about this enigmatic beauty, Adam stayed frozen in place.

He heard a ragged sigh, saw those shoulders shudder, and watched as she turned around again.

"I don't know what to do," she choked softly.

He did. In one easy move, he swung around the railing, came down the ladder three rungs at a time, and jumped down five feet from her, making her gasp and jerk back.

"Oh my God!" she cried out, looking more appalled and terrified than pleased with her would-be rescuer. "I didn't know you were up there."

"That's why I came down." He took one step closer, searching her face and seeing so much more than he had before. Beautiful bones, ebony eyes, and full lips that didn't need any color to make them more tempting.

But this time he also noticed the slightest shadows under her eyes and a pallor that even her carefully applied makeup didn't cover. That kissable lower lip quivered, and the challenge in her gaze was replaced by something that looked entirely...vulnerable.

That gutted him.

"What's going on?" he asked.

"I...came back." She swallowed as if the next words were hard to say. "I want that job."

That's not what he'd meant, but he nodded. "Okay. What changed your mind?"

She lifted a shoulder, just as casual as could be. But he'd heard her when she thought she was alone, and he knew there was nothing casual about this decision.

"I thought you'd rather starve than work with me," he said.

She closed her eyes and deliberately looked past him, then shifted her gaze to the rest of the place. "Wow, you *do* need help."

"No kidding."

She took a few strides, carefully eyeing everything, like an art critic staring at a not nearly finished canvas and, based on the raised eyebrow and slight sniff, finding it wanting.

"Did you talk to someone?" he asked. "Realize what a great opportunity it is? Or just come to your senses?"

She angled her head, still appraising. "You need light in here," she said. "Light will change everything."

He immediately went to the wall where the bare light switches were, suddenly remembering that he needed to buy coverings for them. But, covered or not, the switches worked. "This'll help."

She scowled when the fluorescents flickered to life in the kitchen area and the light cans in the loft beamed a milky wash over everything.

"Help everyone look their worst," she said, a hand over her eyes as if she needed to shield them. "You need natural light to bring this place alive and fresh air to get rid of that awful smell of sawdust and chemicals." She squinted up to the shutters. "There's a stunning view out there," she added. "You need to remove those hideous window coverings."

Which he didn't have time or money to do. "Jadyn," he said, letting her name slide off his tongue. "Do you think I didn't hear you practically sobbing in desperation when you thought I wasn't here?"

"Sobbing? Because you weren't here?" She cocked a brow. "Wow, you do think highly of yourself."

"And you are quite skilled at not answering questions, which you're going to have to answer before we work together."

"Why? What difference does it make why I'm here as long as you get what you want?"

He considered the question and decided it deserved honesty, even if he wasn't getting any from her. "Because I need to trust anyone I work with in any capacity."

"You can trust me."

It was his turn to lift a dubious brow. And he could have sworn she paled.

She exhaled in resignation. "I came back because I decided I'd been too hasty. And I didn't sob, not even close. You must have been hearing things. And I don't know what other probing questions I'm not answering, but you're going to have to pay me in cash."

"Why?"

"Because that's how I work. Fifteen percent on top of any purchase you make that I recommend and a fair hourly rate for my design ideas."

"I guess."

She narrowed her eyes at him. "Is that a yes or a no?"

Jeez. "It's a maybe."

"Not good enough. Cash or no deal."

"Fine, cash. Anything else?"

"Yes, one more thing." She put a hand on the first rung of the ladder and swung herself up. "No more personal questions. None. Zero. Ever."

Adam didn't move a muscle, stunned and speechless as she started to make her way up the ladder.

When he didn't respond, she turned and looked over her shoulder. "Of me, I mean. I can ask you anything I want."

He felt his jaw unhinge. "How is that fair?"

"It's not about fair. I'm looking for inspiration. And you're looking at my rear end. Stop it."

Blinking, he shifted his gaze up. "Sorry. It was right in front of me. What do you mean you're looking for inspiration?"

"For the design. I'm not just going to throw paint on the walls, beds in the loft, and a few cabinets in that hole you think is a kitchen, you know." She kept going until she reached the top, pulling herself up the last rung and now standing where he had been when he'd watched her come in.

How had that happened?

"You're not? But that's what I want you to do."

"But that's not what *I* do." Holding the railing that ran along the loft, she inhaled slowly and took a long, leisurely look around. Up and down, back and forth, ceiling to floor. "Wow."

"I know, a lot of work."

"A lot of potential, too," she said. "What's your budget?"

"Cheap."

She shot him a look.

"Or a little higher," he added, still looking up, confounded by the fact that she'd switched places with him and suddenly was calling the shots when *he'd* hired *her*.

"We'll start with an in-depth interview, and then I'll need to go think and sketch and come up with some preliminary ideas."

Preliminary? "I don't have time for that. I have to finish this place in three weeks. Two weeks and six days now. We need to shop. You need to shop. I need to buy lumber for the stairs and hang doors and—"

"Get rid of those horrifying shutters."

He dug for control. "The shutters stay. I don't have the manpower to get them down."

She started walking along the loft, silent, still assessing. For a *preliminary* design. What the hell had he gotten into?

"Let's start with why you want to do this so badly," she said. "I need to understand you before I understand your environment."

"No, you don't." Because he had no intention of going there.

But she just gave a light laugh like...she was in control now and he was going wherever she wanted him to.

Chapter Five

S he didn't want to admit how excited she was, so Jane kept it very cool as she continued a slow and thorough walk through a dream project.

"It's certainly a blank canvas," she said as they both ended up in the middle of the living area. "Do you have plans I can see? Floor plans or architectural design?"

He snorted. "My grandfather and some friends built this place in the late 1940s from wood they cut from the mountains. Pretty sure there was no *architecture* involved."

"Really?" Her eyes widened. "So much history."

"It was once a place to store small boats, then that business died down, and it became just a big warehouse and dumping ground for shit people didn't want anymore."

"Kind of like the kids you're trying to bring here."

He drew back at the comment. "I don't think of it that way."

She looked around for somewhere to sit, seeing nothing but a low workbench. "Do you have some paper, Adam? I need to make some notes and sketch ideas."

"Really? It's not that big a job." His frustration was palpable, but she ignored it.

"But you want it done right."

He didn't argue with that, but disappeared around the corner into the kitchen while she got comfortable on the bench, peering up at the windows she couldn't wait to make bare and bright. History. Yes, this place was oozing it. But how to capture that?

She'd start with the history of the owner.

When he came back, she scooted over to make room for him. "Tell me about your family."

He practically choked. "What does that have to do with buying bunk beds and shower curtains?"

She gave him a very light elbow. "Humor me."

"Okay, okay. My family." He thought for a second, then said, "My grandpa Max Tucker was one of the founders of this town, and like I said, he built this place. He also built the house that's now the watersports business, and a restaurant on the west side that's now on the bridge."

She jotted a few notes. "Oh, so you must come from a wealthy family."

He looked skyward. "So not. Some of the founders, one in particular, was rich, but Grandpa barely made ends meet. The rest of my family's just chugging along."

"Are they all here?" she asked.

"My dad owns No Man's Land, and my sister just moved back from New York. She's starting her own restaurant here. You met my brother, Zane, who started A To Z and let me buy in as a partner when I left the Coast Guard. And that's the whole family."

She frowned, not sure if she should ask, but it seemed like such an obvious question. "Where's your mother?"

"Somewhere in LA, far as I know. My parents are divorced."

Something nearly imperceptible tightened in his

voice, making her immediately suspect this subject was a sore one. Which meant it was probably the portal to understand what made him tick, which was how she would come up with a design theme for his boathouse.

"I see," she said, adding the word *mother* to her notes.

"You see?" The edge in his voice sharpened, but he tried to hide it with a laugh. "Do I have Martha Stewart or Sigmund Freud on the job?"

"Neither, but knowing about you will help me create something that reflects your personality."

"My personality? Simple. If it can be climbed, rafted, camped on, or enjoyed outside, I like it." He gave her a long look that sent an unexpected flutter through her. A look that made her think he'd like to enjoy *her* outside. "And what I'd really like is if kids can sleep and live here in three weeks," he added.

"All right, but will you answer personal questions?"

"Only if I get to ask one."

"It's not my building," she answered quickly. "And that would be breaking the rules."

He searched her face for a moment, the scrutiny intense and hot. "I can't do that unless you share back. Information this personal is a give-and-take, don't you think?"

"No. You're the client, I'm the designer."

"But I need to trust you, and I have trust issues."

"Who doesn't?" she shot back, getting warmer under his direct gaze. "So tell me about your mother."

"When you tell me about your childhood."

She gave a mirthless laugh. "You show me yours, I'll show you mine. You really want to play stupid kid games?"

He leaned closer, putting one hand on the bench

between them, so close his fingertips grazed her jeans. "I don't want to play games at all. I have a job to do. Either you do it or don't, but I do not want to sit here and talk about mommy issues."

"So you have them?" she replied.

"You want to know about my mother?" he asked. "Is that going to get you into action and doing the job?"

"Maybe."

He didn't answer, but inched back, crossing his arms in a classic pose of self-protection.

"She left when I was fifteen," he said, his voice completely emotionless. "My little sister was eleven. My twin brother had just gotten over a lifetime of fighting asthma and finally started sports. My dad gave up his dream of being a guitarist and accepted that he would be a short-order cook and diner owner his whole life. But my mom? She couldn't give up her dreams."

There was something dead about his tone. Like he'd recited the story. Or hated it.

"What were her dreams?"

"She wanted to be an actress. No, *no*," he corrected quickly. "She wanted to be a star. She didn't want to be Vicky Tucker, so she became Tori Remington."

"Tori Remington?" The name instantly conjured a perky smile, shiny blond hair, and the beautiful maternal face of America's favorite TV sitcom family. "The mom on *Mother May I?* I remember that show. It was hilarious how perfect she was in the face of all that boy chaos."

He closed his eyes. "Exactly."

Then what he was telling her started to make sense. "That's why your parents got divorced? Because she got so famous on TV?"

"It wasn't quite like that, more because she got the part and wanted to go to LA. Then she became a star by pretending to be the mother of a fake family instead of the one she, you know, had in her own home." Bitterness slipped through every word. Bitterness and anger.

"Why didn't you all go with her? I mean, that's a pretty big job, being a TV star."

"Good damn question."

She leaned forward, sensing a breakthrough. Was this why he wanted to help kids? If so, she'd turn the place into the most comforting cave of warmth she could. "Then answer it."

"My parents didn't want to raise us in LA," he said, looking away. "My dad didn't want to leave Eagle's Ridge. We visited her, but she was always on the set or doing interviews and surrounded by a bunch of hangers-on. I'm not sure she wanted us there, to be honest. In any case, she left, and we survived."

But that lifelessness in his voice made her wonder just how well they'd survived. "So you don't trust people because of that."

"Would you if your mother had done that?"

Her mother had done so much worse, it was laughable. "And this is why you want to help troubled kids? To make up for that pain?"

He frowned at her, shaking his head again. "I don't want to do this," he said. "I just want to buy some freaking furniture."

"Okay, if you answer the question. Why is this project so important to you?"

He just stared at her, silent.

"Adam, if you can't answer that, then I can't even begin to design the kind of place that you can be proud of or happy to walk into. I have to have some insights, because that's how I work. Didn't you say you were a rescue swimmer?"

He nodded, nothing but skepticism and maybe a little wariness in his eyes.

"Well, didn't you have to know certain things before you could do your job well? Things about the tide, the weather, the...I don't know, the speed to go down a rope to grab someone. Isn't that right?"

"Yes." He still had that detached tone she didn't understand.

"So help me out here. Why is this project so important? What are you trying to do with it? Does it have to do with your work in rescue? Are you rescuing these kids?"

For a long time, several heartbeats or more, he stared at her. "You know what?" he finally said, standing up. "This was a bad idea."

She blinked up at him. "Why?"

"Because it was. I can pay you for today and your, um, ideas."

She laughed softly. "I didn't give you any."

"I mean, I know you obviously need a job and are hiding out and afraid someone will find out who you are, which is why I can't ask questions and you want cash, and for all I know, Jadyn McAllister isn't even your name."

She felt the blood drain from her face and prayed he didn't notice.

"I'm right, aren't I?"

She answered with a noisy swallow.

After a second, he blew out a breath. "Yeah, you better go. What's your hourly rate? I can pay you for a day."

The statement made the blood rush back into her cheeks with an embarrassed vengeance.

"No need," she said, standing up, mustering every ounce of professionalism she'd ever developed over the years. "I had fun walking through this place, and I'll be thinking about your design if you change your mind."

"Do you have a card?" he asked, probably just to be polite. Or maybe to put her even more on the spot.

"Actually, no. I'm not sure how long I'll be in town." With a tight smile, she scooped up her bag and walked across the empty boathouse to the door, hating how much she hoped he'd stop her.

But of course he didn't.

Adam was still seething as darkness fell. Not that he'd know it was dark, because he still had the shutters that she wanted taken off...but not until she knew every deep, dark emotion of his life and refused to share anything about herself.

He hoisted the door he'd been sanding off the worktable and carried it to the bathroom, which was sorely in need of a door. He'd spent all day on the frame, fuming mostly, taking his frustrations out on nails and wood, wishing he could hike and escape to the mountains for some peace.

"You in here?" a woman's voice called into the boathouse, and Adam hesitated for one split second, thinking it was Jadyn.

But it was his sister, of course. "I'm behind this door, Bailey." He poked his head around the wood. "Follow me to the bathroom."

"Who could resist an offer like that?" She tossed a bag on the floor, and he heard her booted steps cross the wood. "Wow, you are behind."

"Tell me something I don't know." He turned to lean the door on the wall and grab the hardware.

"Mmm." The noncommittal response was out of character for his feisty, opinionated sister, making him glance at her to get a read. But she just looked happy, as she had been since Ryder Westbrook came into her life and she put her troubles in New York behind her.

"I can do it," he assured her.

"I heard you hired help."

"Ford's coming this weekend to work on the stairs."

"Ford Garrison? Oh, I'll have to tell Ryder."

He narrowed his eyes. "If Ryder needs help expanding the airport, tell him to get his own construction workers. Ford's coming here for me. Oh, and he doesn't want anyone to know he's in town."

"So you tell me the minute I walk in," she said on a laugh.

"I trust you." He managed to slide the door into the hinge. "Can't say that about everyone I've met lately, that's for sure," he muttered under his breath.

"Oooh. That sounds intriguing." She reached for the mallet on the floor, anticipating his need. But that was Bailey, unafraid to jump in and get her hands dirty. Unlike some women, who just wanted to *ask questions* and *take notes*.

He tapped the pin into place. "How'd you manage to tear yourself away from the great and powerful Ryder Westbrook?"

She helped steady the door. "Haven't you figured out by now that the Ryder you thought you knew in high school isn't the real guy?"

"He wasn't valedictorian, captain of the football team, and loaded?"

"He's so much more than what you see on the surface. He told you about the search-and-rescue team he's going to start at the airport, right? He asked you to consider helping him as a reserve rescuer."

Adam closed his eyes. Ryder had asked, and Adam hadn't answered. He still wasn't sure about that. "Yeah, he did."

"We're happy, Adam," she said softly. "I've never been happier, as a matter of fact."

"I'm glad," he said honestly, ceasing his search for the other pin to look into his sister's blue eyes. They were more like Dad's than Mom's, he mused. And they were sparking with an inner joy that he'd rarely seen before. "He's been really good for you."

"Yeah, he has." She got the pin and handed it to him. "Anyway, I came over to help Dad with the dinner rush because Mandy has the night off and Brenda couldn't come in."

"That was nice of you." She'd worked briefly at the restaurant when she returned to Eagle's Ridge, but now she had her own place and was as involved with the renovation of it as he was with this. "Why couldn't Brenda come in?" he asked.

"She went up into the mountains with some friends to take sunset pictures."

"Oh…okay." He screwed up his face. "Brenda went on a hike on a Monday night instead of work? What the hell?"

She laughed. "The woman can have a life, Adam. She isn't chained to the diner. Although…"

"Although what?" Adam asked, finally finishing the bottom hinge. "If you're going to start that lunacy about Dad and Brenda again, I'm going to—"

"I think she's on to something." Zane's voice preceded him by two steps, and then even the boathouse seemed a little smaller when his sizable brother walked in.

54

To this day, Adam marveled a bit at how Zane had gone from a sickly kid who couldn't go outside or climb mountains or jump in the river without an asthma attack, to a dude who was, as Jadyn had pointed out within minutes of meeting him, bigger than Adam. And nicer.

"What makes you say that?" Bailey asked.

"I had dinner with Dad last night," Zane said, crossing the room to inspect the door. "He talked about Brenda...a lot."

"Well, they're friends," Adam said. "They've worked together forever."

"And she was Mom's closest friend," Bailey added, her voice indicating that she was making a point. Both men looked at her, and she shrugged. "Brenda's staring down the barrel of fifty-five years old, and I think she wants more in life than just serving up HALOs and Master Guns." She looked skyward. "God, I hate those stupid military names."

"Hey," Adam said. "Don't mess with tradition. It's what put Eagle's Ridge on the map."

"And tourism is keeping us there," Zane added, crossing his arms over his mighty chest. "Which is what brings me here."

Adam stepped away from the door, checking it out. "I don't think bare wood has to be painted, does it?"

Bailey snorted. "Uh, yeah, it does."

Zane was looking around, his focus landing on the empty kitchen. "You're really behind."

"So I've been told." Irritation danced up his spine. "I'll get it done."

"How are things working out with the designer?" Zane asked.

"They're not." Adam marched across the room to replace tools in the box and start cleaning up.

"Is that who you can't trust?" Bailey asked.

He closed his eyes and swore softly.

"I'll take that as a yes," she added, nothing but smug satisfaction in her voice. "Details, please."

Not a chance. "Zane, what's the problem?"

"How do you know there is one?" Bailey asked, the tiniest bit of disbelief in her voice. "How is it that you two can silently communicate? You've done it your whole lives, you know, and it ticks me off."

They both ignored her, probably more out of habit than not caring about their little sister, because they did.

"You figure out the schedule for this weekend's tours?" Zane asked.

Of course not. He hadn't walked into the office all day. "I'll get to them in the morning," he promised. "There's three, if I recall."

"You're going to have to take a run or two?"

"I can't," he said. "Ford's coming in from Virginia to help me build stairs. I won't let him do that alone."

"He prefers alone," Zane said.

"True, but I need him to be here," Adam replied.

"So, what happened with the designer?" Bailey interjected, obviously refusing to let the subject die. "Brenda mentioned someone really pretty had you tied in knots."

He tamped down a grunt of frustration, which would have just made his sister more curious. "She didn't work out, Bailey. She's...not what I'm looking for."

"Yeah, I heard she wore makeup, so not your type."

He glared at her. "Do you mind?"

"What *I* mind is that we have three tours this weekend and no guide," Zane said, on a completely different wavelength.

"She told Brenda she's ditching a guy back in Miami

and hiding out here." Bailey looked a little smug with all her information.

"Which is amazing that Brenda found that out since Jadyn has a no-personal-questions rule, but that doesn't stop her from asking them." Adam heard the disgust in his own voice.

"What about the tour this weekend?" Zane insisted.

"But you did ask her?" Bailey continued.

Adam looked from one sibling to the other, not liking either of these parallel conversations. "I hired Holly, and if she can start this weekend, I'm giving her at least one of the tours. You can do one, Zane. That leaves one white water tour on Sunday, and it's small, only four people."

"I can't do Sunday," Zane said.

"Convenient," Adam replied, only half teasing.

"It's not about the bet, Adam," Zane shot back. "You think I would have sent you a designer if I cared that much about winning?"

"But he doesn't like the designer," Bailey added. "Too inquisitive. And makeup-y."

He dropped his head back and closed his eyes. "You two are killing me."

"A sibling's job," Bailey said, but she came closer and slipped her arm around him. "I can take the Sunday tour. If I can bring Ryder and you pay me double time."

"Done," he agreed, pointing at Zane. "You happy now?"

"I just have one more issue."

Oh boy. He really didn't like the way Zane said that.

"It's good news and bad news. Which do you want first?"

"Just tell me what the hell it is, Zane, and don't make me wager a guess."

Zane exhaled, running a hand through his thick dark hair. "I had to say yes, Bro. It was too much money. It could make our entire month. I booked a big tour. Big. Like forty people on a corporate retreat. I'm bringing in some freelance guides, but it'll be all hands on deck for a week."

"That's great, Zane." Those kinds of events came in once, maybe twice, a season, and the profit was insane. "What's the bad news?"

"They want preseason and start to arrive a week from Friday."

He let that hit his brain like a punch. "That's in ten days. So, our season starts in full swing in ten days?"

Zane looked truly apologetic. "Look, I know how much this boathouse means to you, but when you see the bottom line, you'll get it. It's like an extra month of summer for us. I was on the spot because it was us or North Snake Adventures, and I hate to lose to those guys. The date's not negotiable, but the price was, and I got a small fortune."

But it cost Adam eleven precious days.

"You'll have this finished easily next year in time for that season," Zane said.

"Like hell I will."

Bailey squeezed his arm. "You will, Adam."

"I'll have it done in time for this season. You can bet on it."

Zane just laughed. "I already have."

Chapter Six

J ane started the day optimistic she'd find something for work in the colorful, eclectic tourist town of Eagle's Ridge, but as the morning slid into afternoon, she was beginning to feel a heavy weight of hopelessness on her chest.

She'd been given at least ten paper applications to work in several restaurants, clothing stores, a pet shop, and one auto place called Nuts 'n' Bolts. In addition, several businesses had directed her to online applications. There was work in Eagle's Ridge during the summer season if a person was willing to give her real name, Social Security number, and show a driver's license or ID that matched the name she was using.

Should she risk it and call herself Lydia Swann... after she'd already given another fake name to people in town? Or just try one more place with the hope that some lovely storeowner would say, *Sure, start today, we pay in cash*.

Of course, she'd *had* a cash-paying job and lost it. But she so wanted to do justice to that space. She wanted to coax magnificence out of it, and she knew how to do that. She just had to start with the man who owned it. Why did he have to be so reluctant and cagey about answering simple questions?

She didn't have to make the design about him, but he never really gave her a chance to get there. Overnight, instead of mentally redecorating her dingy motel room, she'd gone back to that boathouse a thousand times in her brain. She scrounged up paper and worked on several layouts for the loft, the kitchen, and the living room. She imagined a mural on one wall, light pouring in from the windows, and something so inviting up in that loft that the little residents wouldn't want to leave. But, no. Adam Tucker had fired her before she started.

On a sigh, she turned a corner to start the next street, but slowed her step at the sight of a precious one-story, rustic-looking building with a gabled roofline trimmed in red and matching red wooden and glass doors.

To her utter delight, it was the library, and it looked like the perfect place to sit and review the applications, and maybe get access to the Internet and those online apps. As she took the two steps to the entryway, she already imagined the rough-hewn wood and rustic feel of a cozy small-town library.

She was pleasantly surprised to be wrong. Clearly, someone with excellent design skills had recently renovated the space, which was airy and expansive, topped with vaulted ceilings.

Behind the front desk, a woman looked up and greeted her with a quick smile, brushing back a lock of dark blond hair to reveal pretty, if completely unadorned, eyes. Well, she'd heard they were natural around here, but this one was truly an untapped beauty.

"Hello," the woman said. "Can I help you?"

"Well, I don't know." Jane rounded a small table

filled with local flyers and information. "Do you have a computer I can use?"

"We do," she said. "We don't get many requests for it, but each of our study rooms has a computer and Internet access. Will that work?"

"It sure will. Can I book one for an hour?"

The woman laughed lightly. "I haven't been the librarian here for very long," she said, "but we haven't had a rush on the rooms yet. You can stay as long as you like. Come on, I'll take you back."

"Thank you." Jane smiled gratefully as the woman came around the desk, smoothing a long sweater that covered narrow hips and hung shapelessly over black slacks.

She had a lovely figure and face, but it was all hidden and downplayed, Jane thought as she sneaked a second look.

"I'm Harper Grace, head librarian." She extended her hand. "And you are?"

"Ja—Jadyn McAllister," she replied, shaking hands.

"I'm new to Eagle's Ridge, so I have to introduce myself to everyone. You?"

"I'm just…passing through," Jane said.

The other woman smiled, her lips the tiniest bit glossy from nothing but ChapStick, Jane presumed. "And you stop in the library? I'm honored." They reached a small door, and Harper produced a key ring to unlock it. "Just holler if you need anything else," she said. "Of course, no food and drink allowed."

"Of course." She doubted this librarian ever broke a rule.

When she opened the door, Jane was instantly happy with her decision. The room had a window with a mountain view, a desk and comfortable chair, and a desktop computer with a printer. "This is fantastic, thanks."

"Great. Help yourself to the printer and paper, but we do charge ten cents a page, on the honor system."

Jane nodded. "You can trust me."

Harper's smile was tentative but reached pale gray eyes, making them gleam as much as if she'd spent half an hour on makeup. "I'm sure I can trust you, Ms....McAllister, was it?"

No. "Yes." Jane swallowed, hating that she had to follow a promise of trust with a lie.

A few minutes later, Jane was settled in with the applications strewn in front of her and an online application open on the screen. More lies waiting to be told, she thought.

No, forget lying. A job without legit ID was going to be impossible.

Regret bubbled up when her mind went back to Adam Tucker again. Maybe she should have just slapped a coat of paint on the walls, helped him buy some unremarkable furniture, picked out a few area rugs, and called it a day. Why did she have to be such a perfectionist?

Oh, she knew why. Because if she had been a more perfect child, maybe her mother would have loved her more, and then maybe child services wouldn't have taken Jane away and hidden her in a "safe" home where nothing and no one was really all that safe.

It didn't take a PhD in psychology to figure out why Jane McAllen was who she was, and if that man wanted her to be his designer, he'd have to let her do it the right way and make it perfect.

A smile pulled at her lips when she thought about the incredible potential that big old boathouse had. And that smile grew wistful when she thought of Adam Tucker with his intense blue-green gaze and strong, masculine physique. It wouldn't have been awful to spend time working side by side with him, inhaling the musk of carpentry and fresh air that clung to him, verbally sparring and occasionally letting their hands brush.

Oh, it would all be so tempting, tense, even, but not a bit awful.

Pushing away the blank applications, she made room on the desk for the sketches she'd made last night on the tiny note paper from the Hideaway. Taking a small stack of paper from the printer, she counted ten sheets and pulled out her pencil.

On each page, she sketched a different part of the boathouse—a wall of the main room, the loft, the kitchen, and then the living area. She even made some design choices for the bathroom.

Thinking about the ambience and layout, she looked out the window and studied the dramatic lines of the mountains, the deep green of the trees, and the rich earthy tones of soil. Spring buds threatened to burst into full yellow bloom on the low side of the mountains, broken by bright patches of green grass.

Yes, the color palette would be a breeze. But it was more than color...it was the vibe, the impact, the message she wanted to send to these unlucky kids who got lucky for one week.

And that, she realized with a jolt, was the real reason she'd wanted the job. And the reason she wanted the finished product to be so amazing.

What Adam didn't know was that she connected with those kids far better than he ever could, despite his absentee mother. He had a family—a brother he worked with, a father nearby, a sister who had come home to nest.

And he couldn't even explain why it was an important project. Was it a tax write-off? A money maker? A strong sense of altruism? Or were his motives deeper?

She sighed heavily and closed her eyes and started to imagine that space finished in the colors of the mountains and earth, the lines of each room highlighted by sunlight pouring in from those glorious high windows.

The furniture would be rustic and wild, like the landscape, and rich with textures that were both rough and inviting, like the world around it. A zing of excitement rushed through her as she grabbed another stack of paper and ventured out to find the librarian again.

"What are the chances of me snagging any colored markers?" she asked Harper, who answered by pulling open her drawer and producing a box with a smile.

"Anything else?" she asked.

"You're amazing," Jane said on a laugh, taking the markers. "Thank you." As she started walking away, her gaze landed on one of the brochures on the table, announcing the Eagle's Ridge Founder's Day. Picking it up, she flipped the page open to read about an event that…happened four weeks ago.

"Some of those flyers are woefully outdated, I'm afraid," Harper said from behind the desk. "It's next on my list to redo that display."

"Wasn't Max Tucker one of the founders?" Jane asked. "The man who built that boathouse on the river?"

Harper gave an apologetic look. "I'm so new, I don't know the history. There's a small section of books on Eagle's Ridge over there near reference, if you want them."

"I do," she said brightly, more ideas forming as she headed that way. "I'd very much like to look at them."

The reference books were mostly about the Pacific Northwest in general and the Blue Mountains and Snake River area in particular. But there was one tiny paperback called *Eagle's Ridge: Military Town* that looked like it had been locally produced that had a brief history of Eagle's Ridge, naming Max Tucker as a founder, along with three other veterans of World War II. There were a few sections on how the town grew after World War II with a strong family emphasis on the military service.

Ideas started to form, designs took shape, and Jane headed back to waste the afternoon on a job she'd never get. But the work soothed and distracted her, and when the sweet librarian tapped on the door and told her the library was closing in five minutes, Jane had no regrets about the lost time. It was what she did…too bad nobody wanted her ideas.

Sometimes it felt like nobody wanted *her*.

Adam Tucker didn't know the meaning of the word *quit*, and he wasn't about to learn it now. He closed the gate of his truck on the boxes of inexpensive, unassembled bunk beds he'd just bought and decided that sleep and giving up were for losers.

He'd build one of the damn beds before Ford got here on Friday, or maybe the two of them could put them together over some beers.

He could do this. He *had* to do this. It was well over two years since he'd left the Coast Guard, well over two years since he left the home of Nadine Butcher and apologized for not saving her son. Well over two years since Nadine came running out to the driveway, tears streaming.

Do something for boys like my Dalton, Nadine had said. *Make them more like you and less lost.*

He would never forget the mourning mother's plea and the way the unexpected compliment had twisted his heart. As a teenager, Adam could have gone the same route that Dalton Butcher had, he thought. When his mother left, Adam drank. He smoked weed. He got in trouble…once or twice.

That was all it took for Sam Tucker to rein him in and settle his ass down, reminding him that he came from a long line of military men who didn't screw up their lives. Since he'd been a kid, he wanted to be a Coast Guard rescue swimmer, just like his best friend, Wyatt, wanted to be a HALO-jumping Navy SEAL. They'd both realized their dreams, and Adam had saved over a hundred drowning people in his career.

And lost one. The memory of that boy slipping out of his grasp was never far from his mind. It was so close, in fact, that he'd yet to complete another rescue since that day.

He'd left the Coast Guard and come here. He'd guided boats and made sure no one drowned, but a real rescue? Swimming against the tide, with someone in a rescue lock, fighting for a life?

He hadn't *had* to…but he wasn't sure he could if put to the test. Part of him thought he couldn't ever do it again. The other part hoped to hell he wasn't tested.

He hit the accelerator and turned onto the main road that led back into Eagle's Ridge, the memories pulling him down way further than the annoying errand he just finished. At least he had somewhere for Ford to sleep, since his apartment was small and they would have been cramped as hell.

Now he had to...*stop*.

He narrowed his eyes at the tacky sign for the Hideaway Hotel coming up on the right. Was Jadyn still staying at that dump? Or had her need for cash forced her to go somewhere even seedier? An unexpected punch in the gut hit hard as he thought of her in a dire situation. Because he'd been a jerk and turned her out when she asked too many questions.

So maybe he didn't like her approach to his problem, but she was a solution. And he'd sent her away.

Yes, she was a pain with all her questions. Yes, she was an enigma who refused to answer any. Yes, she was distractingly beautiful and hauntingly vulnerable. Who needed to deal with all that when he was pushed against the wall for time?

He did.

Adam hit the brakes, turned the wheel, and pulled into the parking lot of the Hideaway. Just to check on her. Maybe offer the money she'd refused to take. How about an apology for acting like a jerk when she asked personal questions that he didn't want to answer?

Yeah, he owed her that, but how was he going to find her?

The way he'd find any guest—at the front desk. But as he pulled up to the one-story office along the side of the motel, the first thing he noticed was an Eagle's Ridge PD cruiser parked right outside.

Not that unusual for this dump, which was probably the site of more than one crime per week. But still. On a weekday at eleven in the morning?

Curiosity piqued, he parked and headed in, seeing a familiar face the minute he entered the undersized reception area. Lieutenant Michael Stonecipher was a few years older than Adam, a kid who'd grown up a few streets over from the Tuckers. He'd been a cop in town for well over a decade now and had a reputation for being fair to the locals and tough on the tourists who caused trouble.

"Hey, Adam," he said, looking up from his phone while his partner, a woman Adam didn't know, spoke to the person behind the desk. "What are you doing here?"

"Better question." Adam took a few steps closer. "What are you doing here?"

"Robbery."

"Alleged," the man behind the desk corrected. "That guest could be lying."

"Or your maid could, Johnny," Mike tossed back.

"I'll be with you in a moment," Johnny said to Adam.

"S'okay," Adam replied, then turned to Mike. "Who got robbed?"

"A guest claims the maid stole some money, but the owner here thinks the guest is making that up."

A guest. A *lying* guest. A tendril of worry pulled at his chest. "Do you know who it is?" he asked.

Mike looked up from his phone at the question. "Are you involved in any way, Adam?"

"No, no. I know someone staying here, that's all."

A flicker of surprise crossed muddy-brown eyes, but before he could respond, his partner turned from the desk. "We need to get started, Mike," she said. "We'll talk to every guest that's in the motel to see if they lost anything. Check ID and make a list of who's here and who's not."

"My guests are going to love that, Officer Crawford," Johnny complained noisily.

Well, Adam knew one who probably wouldn't.

"Just give me the list," Officer Crawford demanded.

Adam didn't really know what was going on here and didn't care. But everything in him wanted to get to Jadyn before they did.

"Here you go." She handed the list to Mike just as he pressed his phone to his ear to answer a call.

"Hang on," he said, putting the paper on the counter top next to him, just a foot from where Adam stood, and turning to talk into the phone. Adam didn't even hesitate, glancing down the page at a list of about a dozen names.

Jadyn McAllister, Room 16, jumped right out at him.

"What did you need, sir?" the man behind the desk asked him.

"Nothing. I wanted to ask about… It's not important when you're dealing with this. I'll come back." With a nod to Mike, Adam slipped out, jumped into his truck, and drove along the building until he reached Room 16. Something told him she wouldn't want to talk to the police or show ID, or maybe she was the guest who'd been robbed. Either way, he wanted to help her. He owed her that much.

He knocked twice and waited, instantly hearing footsteps on the other side of the door. But she didn't answer, so he knocked again and kept his face in front of the peephole so she could see and recognize him.

"Jadyn?"

Still no answer.

"Are you the guest who was robbed today?"

After a second, the chain unlatched, and she opened the door an inch. He could see only a section of her face, but it was enough to make him draw back a little in surprise. He recognized her, of course, but she was so different. So natural. So completely real. And something in his chest shifted a little.

"What are you talking about, and what are you doing here?" she asked.

"A guest was robbed, and the cops are here, and they're about to come door to door and check ID."

That was enough to make her eyes widen and let the door slip open a little more so he could see all of her face. Why would she ever cover that perfection with a speck of makeup?

"Do I have to talk to them?" she asked. "Can't I just not answer the door?"

He could see she wore a long T-shirt and those skintight leggings some women wore as pants now, so she was dressed enough to talk to someone at her door. "I guess, but why wouldn't you?"

A little bit of blood drained from her face.

"Are you in trouble, Jadyn?"

She held his gaze, searching his face, no doubt debating how much to trust him. "No. I'm just a very private person, and I wasn't robbed, and I have nothing to say to the police. Is that why you're here?"

"I was in the neighborhood."

She gave a quick, dry laugh.

"I bought some beds." He pointed with his thumb over his shoulder. "Bunk beds. They're in my truck."

Her gaze shifted over his shoulder. "I don't see any bunk beds."

"Yet to be assembled."

She inched the door wider. "You bought prefab unassembled beds for that gorgeous space?" She sounded disgusted which, for some reason, made him smile. Because she cared about his boathouse, even after he'd made her leave.

"My designer wasn't available for consult."

"Your designer was fired for asking too many questions."

"I'm sorry."

The simple apology softened her features, and he lifted his hand to let his knuckle graze her chin. "Why?"

"Why was I fired? Only you know the answer to that."

He rubbed lightly, loving the insane smoothness of her skin and the way his touch put the tiniest glimmer in her eyes. "Why do you wear makeup on this indescribably beautiful face?"

He felt a little breath escape her lips. Maybe a sigh. A laugh. A soft puff of disbelief. "How about why are you here when I was already fired from the job?"

"I'm…desperate." He was, really. "My timeline was cut. My patience is gone. My help is… Do you really think the space is gorgeous?"

A siren coming closer to the motel kept her from answering, and she stepped back.

"Jadyn, why are you hiding? Seriously, are you in trouble?"

Her lower lip trapped under her front teeth, she shook her head, giving a non-answer that made him crazy.

"Tell me and I'll help you."

"I can't. You have to trust me that I cannot tell you why I…" She glanced over his shoulder in the direction of the sirens. "I need to leave."

There was just enough low-grade panic in her voice to squeeze his chest. "Get your stuff. Come with me."

She hesitated for a second, just a split second, and then he saw her make the decision that he'd seen on the faces of a hundred near-drowning victims. The decision to let go of whatever they were holding on to for dear life and take his hand.

She let him inside the tiny room, where the bed was made, the top of the dresser was empty except for a stack of papers, and a bag was packed and sitting on a chair.

"Looks like you're already ready to go."

"I keep it that way so I can..." The siren screamed louder.

"Maybe they caught the guy and won't come over here at all," he suggested.

"You think?" Desperation cracked her voice.

"I don't know. Is everything you want in there?" He gestured to the suitcase.

"Everything I need. Not my cosmetics."

"You don't need those." He zipped the bag. "Purse? Anything else?"

Snagging her handbag from the back of the door, she snatched the room key and started to follow him. "Oh, wait. I need these." She reached for a stack of white paper, the top sheet covered with streaks of Magic Marker.

"What are they?"

She tapped them together and pressed them to her chest. "Your design plans." She gave him a nudge. "Go, quick."

She did design plans?

"What about my rental car?" She pointed to a little blue compact in the spot outside her room.

"Leave it for now. It won't look like you took off at the first sign of trouble."

Even if she had.

"The room had to be prepaid for two more weeks."

"Then you can come back any time." He gave her a boost into the front seat of the truck and darted around to get in.

"I am so happy to be out of that hellhole," she said, underscoring that by tossing the room key in the cup holder. "But now what do I do?"

"Maybe you should start by trusting me."

"I think I just did."

Chapter Seven

Adam said they were going to his apartment, which would be the "safest" place, and he stayed fairly quiet as they drove there. He drove his oversized, masculine truck with confidence and a steady speed, threading the traffic with ease and occasionally glancing in the rearview as if he half expected the cops to be bearing down on them.

"I didn't have anything to do with any robbery at that motel, if you're worried about that."

"I'm not." He threw her a look, silent for a moment, then he said, "I hate shopping. Did I mention that?"

"You might have." She wasn't sure where he was going with that, but took it as an attempt at small talk. "I happen to love it."

"I'd rather have a root canal."

She laughed. "What is it that you hate so much about it? Do you have difficulty making decisions?"

"No." He tapped the steering wheel with a little pent-up emotion. "I just made a pretty big one, didn't I?"

So much for small talk. "You did," she agreed. "And I appreciate the help."

"Would be nice to know why."

"Why you helped me?"

He threw her a look that she easily interpreted as *don't play games*. "Why you're running from the cops."

"Oh, no. No." She shook her head. "I'm not running from the cops. That is the absolute truth."

"Jadyn." He paused for a moment. "*If* that is your name."

She stared straight ahead, refusing to answer. She'd tell him enough, if she had to, but she would not tell him her name. Or Sergio's. Or Lydia's. He didn't need to know that much.

"Jadyn," he repeated. "We just scooted out of a motel in a big, fat hurry because the cops were crawling all over the place. That is called 'running from the cops' in any book. And one of them is a friend of mine, by the way."

"One of the cops?" She wasn't sure how to take that news.

"Kid I grew up with. Good guy."

She nodded and turned to the window, trying to concentrate on the scenery, which was majestic even on this overcast day. "I need to incorporate grays. I didn't even think about how cloudy it is here all the time."

"Excuse me?"

"In the design," she explained. "I spent all day in the library yesterday and had some real inspiration."

He choked a soft laugh. "You did that *after* I fired you?"

"I did it for fun. For relaxation. Redesigning something to make it the best it can be is my happy place. So, I did it to get my mind off...things." She waited for the barrage of questions about what those things were, but they didn't come. Instead, he nodded with understanding.

"I get that. I hike and raft and climb rocks for fun,

even though I also do it for work. Especially the hiking. I love to go right…" He lowered his head and squinted under the rearview mirror up at the mountains. "There. That ridge. The one this town is named after."

"Eagle's Ridge is named after a real place? That wasn't in the history book I read."

"Unless it was written by my grandfather or one of his cronies, it wouldn't be."

"There was a lot about how the town council formed and the first mayor, and there were some serious arguments about land rights in the early days."

"The big feud, yeah. It was all over land, and a woman, as most feuds are. Everyone in town forgot about it but them. In fact, it only just ended. Kind of."

"Seriously?" She turned in the seat, momentarily fascinated and happy not to be thinking about the cops she wasn't really running from. "How?"

"My sister, Bailey, went and fell hard for John Westbrook's grandson, Ryder." He let out a sigh like he wasn't quite sure about that relationship yet. "We had a big flood a few weeks ago, and the two of them saved my grandpa Max, and I really think that went a long way to convincing John and Grandpa to bury the hatchet, or at least lay the hatchet down in a truce."

"And now they're friends?"

"I wouldn't go that far, but they'll talk if they're in the same room. Anyway," he continued, "you see that big rock jutting out about three-quarters of the way up that mountain?"

She found the spot, which was way high but easy to locate.

"That's the original Eagle's Ridge. The very place our four founding fathers saw a bald eagle when they were looking down over the land that started it all."

"So there was a real eagle that gave the place its name?"

"Oh yeah, and seeing that bird hit those young veterans in the heart, I can tell you, since it was just months after they came home and World War II ended."

"What an incredible story."

"It's an incredible place," he said. "Maybe my favorite on earth. When I'm up there, I'm happy, relaxed, just certain of everything." He gave her an easy smile that did a little something *uneasy* in her chest. All over, to be honest. "That's my, what did you call it? Happy place."

Reaching over, she closed her fingers around his strong, muscular forearm. "Will you take me there?"

"Sure. When the boathouse is finished."

"Now."

He blinked. "Now?" Then he glanced at her leggings and flip-flops. "You can't just park the truck and walk up there, Jadyn. You have to get there by kayak or raft. Well, there are other ways, but you can't handle them."

"Oh." She bit her lip, thinking about what she'd learned in her research about the town. The water was essentially calm to the north of the bridge, but south, there were rocks, drops, and danger. But the calm side was like a lake most days, she'd read. "Is it north of the bridge?"

His eyes flickered with a little amusement, or maybe he was impressed she'd done her homework. "It depends which way you go."

"The safest way."

"So, not the fastest, which would be through the Tapashaw rapids, around a rock garden we locals call the Middle Finger, and not just because the middle rock sticks straight up."

"Then why?"

"Because when you navigate it wrong, you want to flip off Mother Nature because she flipped your flipping kayak," he said on a laugh. "After that, you have to zip down something known as Nakanushee Falls, which can be a little hairy after a heavy rain. But then? You're right under the direct path to the ridge. Still want to go?"

She swallowed. "Is there no other, slightly less adventurous route?"

"Well, yeah." He sighed as if the very thought was unpleasant to him. "You could pick up a hiking path not far from town and meander your way up the mountain with all the other lightweights."

She could hear the challenge in his voice and knew that if she picked the rocks, falls, and rapids, he'd say yes. "I'd just be terrified because... Did you say the kayak would flip?"

"Yeah." He leaned closer and almost let his forehead touch hers to whisper, "I can handle a kayak in my sleep, though."

"And you were a rescue swimmer in the Coast Guard."

A reaction she couldn't read flickered in his eyes, but he instantly moved his gaze back to the mountains before she could interpret it. "They call to you, don't they?"

"Yeah. They do. Who knew a great big hill could do that?"

"Me," he said simply.

"Well, I've never been on a mountain before, so—"

"Never?" He could barely choke the word for the shock.

"Miami, remember?"

"But who... No." He shook his head as if common

sense had just slapped him. "I have so much to do in the boathouse and so little time to do it. And I hadn't expected to be, uh, whisking you away from the law."

"That's not what you did."

He raised a brow. "It's kind of exactly what I did. And I still don't know why."

"If you take me up there, Adam, the lightweight way, I'll tell you."

"Everything?"

Not quite. "Enough."

He closed his eyes for a moment, then gave his head a shake.

"Is that a no?" she asked, surprised at how fast her heart was beating and how much she wanted him to say yes.

"It's a 'I can't believe I'm in this deep.'"

Still holding his arm, she gave it a squeeze. "It's not that deep," she said softly. "Take me up there, Adam. Please. Show me your mountain. Take me to the ridge."

He finally exhaled. "As if I could say no to that."

The one day Adam *didn't* want to hike up to the ridge…and he was on his way. How was that for irony? He wanted to pick up lumber for the stairs and finish installing the last cabinets and get this show on the road, but here he was. Hiking.

He'd grabbed a hiking pack that never left his backseat. Armed with matches, a knife, a tarp, and some protein bars and water, he headed to his "happy place" with a woman whose name he didn't know.

The clouds had gathered a bit to the west, threatening a light rain, but they were moving at a good clip, and he figured they could at least be at the ridge and under the overhang in a shower.

She wasn't talking, but she wasn't winded, either. She was a quick study and learned immediately to watch each step of the sneakers she'd had in her bag. Intent and focused, she was too new to this to look around, and her gaze stayed locked on the rocky path they traveled.

She might never have hiked before, but she held her own and kept up with Adam. He kept waiting for her to tire, but she had strong legs and good endurance.

"You're in good shape," he noted.

"I have a great gym in my building, and I get that incline up to a seven whenever I get on the treadmill."

He grunted softly. "I hate gyms."

"You have Mother Nature's gym," she said.

"So true. We had to work out indoors so often in the Coast Guard, and it always felt so fake to me. I'm not the weight lifter my brother, Zane, is."

"Must be fun growing up with a twin," she mused, taking a break from studying her next step to glance at him.

"I don't know any other life, so I guess it was fun. Zane's a good guy, and I promise you he'll make you some outrageous wager within five minutes of getting to know you."

"He already did," she said. "He told me to talk to you, and he bet me five bucks I'd walk away with a job." She laughed. "I just thought he was funny and nice."

"I'm surprised he hasn't come to collect. Also surprised he bet money. It's usually something more, uh, interesting."

He slowed his step as the path grew rockier and put a hand on her back to make sure she was steady. And because it felt good to touch her, even through the thin down vest he'd lent her.

"Interesting? Like what?"

He snorted. "Like our current bet, which I am obviously not taking seriously enough, or I wouldn't be out here hiking when I should be working." Not that it was about the bet, not at all.

"We'll get to it," she assured him. "What did you bet?"

He just shook his head.

She jabbed him with a teasing elbow. "Come on, tell me."

"It's just…stupid guy stuff."

She grinned up at him. "I want to know what you bet. Not money?"

"Like I said, money is usually too pedestrian for my imaginative brother. Zane likes to bet that the loser has to do something inane. A prank, usually. And trust me, that's how we've always gotten into the most trouble."

"Like what kind of trouble?"

He thought for a second, but already knew the answer. "The worst was probably when we were seniors in high school and I took his bet that he could beat me in a rowing race. I mean, come on. It was Zane, right? I could row circles around him, but…" He closed his eyes. "I wasn't paying attention while Zane got bigger and faster than me. He kicked my butt on that race and won the bet."

"What did you have to do?"

He chuckled, remembering the massive stupidity…and fun they'd had. "I had to superglue a penny over the lock on every door into the school one night, guaranteeing Eagle's Ridge High couldn't open the next day."

She let out a quick laugh. "No! I can't believe you did that."

"Neither could the principal, who had just recently

installed security cameras. Which, I might add, caught my brother laughing his ass off in the parking lot and flipping me pennies. So, it landed both of us in one entire semester of detention, every Saturday for half our senior year." Man, he'd been pissed that they'd missed seeing those cameras.

"Were you in trouble at home?"

He shrugged. Dad had given up on disciplining Adam and Zane by then, with his whole attention on trying to manage fourteen-year-old Bailey. "A little. But you know, that semester of detention ended up creating some pretty great friendships. Besides Zane, we were in with some guys I'm not sure I would have otherwise known. Now they're some of my best friends."

She paused a little, not for a break, but for a soft breath of wonder as they reached the halfway point. They still had a decent hike to the ridge, but this view was stellar, the first real glimpse of how the Snake River wound through Eagle's Ridge, nestled in the valley between the rolling hills that rose to impressive mountains.

"Wow," she whispered. "I need to get out of Florida more often."

He appreciated the view with her, trying to see it through her eyes. Through any eyes it was special, a view he'd loved year-round for his whole life. "Pretty flat there, huh?"

"Our highest elevation is an on-ramp to I-95."

"I would hate that," Adam said. "I need to get up in the mountains to breathe and on that river to relax."

She smiled up at him, nodding and thinking, but he wasn't sure about what. "I see that," she said slowly.

Oh no. "Please don't tell me this is part of your HGTV psychology."

"I *am* looking for inspiration," she told him.

"Well, listen. This is kind of why I shut down the other day. I don't want that boathouse to be about me, okay? I'm just going to run it."

"Okay." But something in her voice told him she wasn't going to back off.

"Plus, the promise was we'd come up here and you'd tell me why you're running, hiding, and using a fake name."

She stumbled on a small rock, her sneaker slipping, making her automatically grab his arm. "Whoa, it can be treacherous up here, huh?"

Treacherous for someone who wanted to change the subject, ask and not answer questions, and who had managed much bigger rocks on the path with ease. He decided to let it go. "I know my way around. You're safe."

"Then back to your bet," she said, a not-so-deft but very definite change of subject. "What did you bet your brother this time?"

He gave her a side-eye, which he could tell she interpreted perfectly.

"Just talk to me for a bit, Adam," she said. "I can't tell you everything while I'm trying to stay vertical and not fall down this mountain."

Oh, she was good at excuses. "Sure," he agreed. "The bet actually goes back to that semester in detention, oddly enough."

"Really?"

He didn't answer as they started walking again, aware that the path got steeper here. "Yeah. Watch this next few hundred feet." He took her hand just in case she slipped for real this time. "Even an experienced hiker can be challenged from here to the ridge."

She nodded, her focus back on her feet, her slender fingers wrapped around his. "Talking helps me concentrate," she said. "Tell me the bet."

"You're relentless." He squeezed her hand. "We have that in common."

"And you're good at changing the subject when you don't want to talk about something." She squeezed back. "We have that in common, too."

For a moment, he just looked at her, meeting her gaze, enjoying the spark of humor in her dark eyes. Just...*liking* her for one long, surprisingly powerful beat of time. Usually when he was at this point in the mountain, his whole focus was out. Looking out over the trees and rocks and down to the valley and river.

But all he wanted to look at now was her, and damn, if she wasn't as pretty as the world around him.

"I'm glad you left your makeup in that motel," he said softly.

One of her brows, dark and arched, lifted. "Now that was an underhanded compliment if I ever heard one."

He kept walking, still holding her hand and enjoying the feel of her slender fingers lost in his much bigger hand. Without thinking too much about it, he lifted her hand and put the lightest kiss on her knuckles. "You're flat-out beautiful. Is that straightforward enough for you?"

He saw her swallow, and then she cast her gaze down, avoiding his intense stare. "Too straightforward for me."

He didn't get her. He just didn't understand this woman, nor did he understand how much he wanted to get her and understand her.

So he continued on the path, silent, guiding her around a small bush that jutted into the path, and ducked under some heavy branches right after that.

"When we were in detention," he finally said, "there was this teacher who monitored Saturdays. She was... attractive."

"Like hot-for-teacher attractive?"

"Like...well, let's put it this way. Her name's Diana Woods, but we just secretly called her Miss Woody. For obvious reasons."

She let out a heartfelt laugh. "Oh, the poor woman."

"I think she might have known about her power over us and used it to her advantage," he said, thinking of that mane of red hair, those sinfully green eyes, and a body that made teenage boys want to cry. Or take really long showers.

"So is she still making life hell for boys at the high school?"

"Yes," he said. "In fact, she's the principal now and, to be fair, still pretty hot. She was only in her twenties back then, so she's barely forty now and somehow still single."

"None of you ever tried to close the deal with her?"

He laughed. "Not that I know of, but someone is now. Last month, a plane went over Eagle's Ridge and wrote 'I love you, Diana' in skywriting."

"And you don't know who?"

"According to Ryder Westbrook, who owns the airport and was part of our detention team, the pilot was paid a lot of money not to reveal who'd hired him. So my inane brother decided that it would be hilarious to add to the small-town buzz by covering Miss Woody's front porch with roses."

"That's the bet?"

He nodded. "That's what the loser will do. So you can see I have to finish that boathouse."

"And don't call her Miss *Woody* if you get caught."

"I'm not going to get caught, because I'm not going to lose," he assured her. "Although today might be a wash on the boathouse project."

"Not a wash, I promise. I'm doing design work in my head with each step we take."

"Great. Well, I'm not installing cabinets with each step we take." He gave her hand a light squeeze. "But it's okay. Right now, I'm where I want to be."

She smiled up at him and then was quiet for a few moments, maybe thinking about that, maybe concentrating as the rocks got much trickier the higher they got. She made no effort to let go of his hand and made only cursory checks of the view as she kept her gaze on her shoes and the stones they covered.

"That's it?" she asked, a little breathless now.

"There's just one more kind of tricky section ahead, then we'll reach the ridge." He tugged her hand gently. "Let me know if you want to stop for water or a break."

"No stopping," she said. "But I meant is that the only reason you're so hell-bent on getting the boathouse finished in three weeks? So you don't have to get busted covering Miss Woody's porch in roses?"

"No, of course not. Once the season starts, we're slammed. It's already starting to pick up, but when the tourists hit this place in early May, A To Z will be humming from morning to night until early September. I won't have time to finish or even deal with the tours." He let out a low groan. "And my deadline's been cut to nine days thanks to one of them coming in early."

"Really? Couldn't you just wait another year, or will the kids be a big source of income?"

He snorted as they reached the big rock he knew was the last major hurdle to the ridge, challenging and dangerous, even for an experienced climber. "We're not going to make much money on the camp. In fact, I'm charging so little, I had to present it to Zane as a charitable write-off." He stopped and pointed to the time- and rain-worn surface of the rock, purposely using his body to block the steep drop behind him. "This is the trickiest part. You have to get over this to get to the ridge, but it's worth it."

"Okay."

"There's a way to do it, but you have to concentrate and use the right technique. Watch me." He slowly put his foot into a crevice in the rock, then another, so familiar with the climb he could do it with his eyes closed. Halfway up, he easily hoisted himself to the top, turning to offer his hand. "I can pull you up. Just try to follow the footholds I used. And whatever you do, don't fall to your right."

She glanced at the slope, which wasn't too steep but was still a long way down on rocks and dirt. "'Kay." She stuck her sneaker in the right place but didn't take his hand. Instead, she placed hers right where his had been and took a deep breath.

"I can pull you, Jadyn."

She shook her head, bit her lip, and pulled hard with a grunt, almost making it, but not quite having the upper-body strength to hoist herself higher.

"Jadyn, it would be easier."

Meeting his gaze, she narrowed her eyes at him. "I want to do it myself," she said. "Just to see if I can."

He smiled at her, giving a slow nod. "Not what I expected from you, glamour girl."

"You don't even know me." She ground the words out as she tried again, gritting her teeth and straining the muscles in her neck as she tried to get up the rock. And failed.

"No, I don't, which is why I brought you up here, since you promised to tell me everything."

She tried again but couldn't make it up. "Damn it," she mumbled.

"Still won't take help?"

"No. I really want to do it myself. Third time's the charm."

"Maybe not. It took me four tries to make it through rescue-swimmer training."

"But you didn't give up, did you?" She raised a challenging brow.

"Didn't even consider it."

"Like I said." She grabbed on hard, her face sheer concentration. "We have more in common than you think."

Adam's chest swelled with an unexpected reaction to that, causing a rush of affection for this woman who was maybe more of his type than he'd even realized.

She fought for strength, pressing her foot firmly against the stone and clinging to the tiny handles nature had made. She turned a little red, bit her lip hard enough to draw blood, and found some strength he'd bet she had no idea she had.

And, son of a gun, she made it, falling right into his waiting arms.

"I did it!" Her whole face lit up with satisfaction, making her even brighter, prettier, and more appealing.

"You did." He hugged her closer, loving the feel of her slender, but strong, body against his. "And your reward is going to be one of the most breathtaking views you've ever seen."

She was looking at him, her eyes dancing, her smile broad, her face flushed from victory. "This view's pretty good, too," she whispered.

"Hey." He tucked his knuckle under her chin. "No changing the subject, pretending to fall, citing psychological studies, *or* flirting with me. You promised to tell me everything."

"I promised to tell you enough."

He shouldn't accept that, and he knew it. But there was pain and fear in her eyes that did something stupid to his heart, so he just nodded. He'd take what he would get and hope "enough" was enough.

Chapter Eight

Adam took Jadyn's hand again as the path wove between thick pine branches, the ground underfoot no more than tiny, slippery rocks.

"Now, listen," he said. "From this point on, it's dangerous until we get to the ridge. The path is narrow, and the drop is very steep. You fall, you die."

She gasped softly. "Seriously?" She ventured a look to her right to confirm that the mountain dropped dramatically, and the only things between a hiker and a fatal fall were a few thin bushes and trees. "Good thing you know how to rescue a person."

"Yeah." He knew how not enthusiastic that sounded, but God, he hated this subject.

"You have saved lives, right?"

"Over a hundred," he said, without fanfare or bragging.

"Have you ever..." She didn't finish the question. But she didn't have to.

He knew exactly what the next question would be and felt his jaw tense in anticipation. He expected honesty from her, and he would have to give it back, right? It wasn't like he'd kept Dalton Butcher's death a secret. His family knew and his closest friends. They just didn't know what it had done to him. They might suspect, but they didn't know.

"Have you ever not been able to rescue someone?" she finally asked.

They followed a sharp veer in the path, and he eased her ahead of him when it grew too narrow for two people. That way, she couldn't see his expression while he didn't answer, and in about ten feet, the view would get them talking about something else entirely.

"Oh my God," she whispered as they rounded the last bend. "That's...wow."

"I know," he said proudly, inching her to the huge flat stone that stuck out like nature had created her own balcony. "It's my million-dollar view."

"I've decorated enough homes with million-dollar views to assure you this is worth much, much more." She scanned from east to west, drinking in the stunning beauty of sky, mountains, trees, river, and a sweet town nestled in the arms of it all. Adam never stood up here and looked out without being awed right down to his bones.

He'd never gone to church, probably never said a prayer in his life, and hadn't spent a lot of time thinking about the Creator of this universe. But up here, he felt close to nature and as holy as an unholy person could feel.

The look on her face, the wonder and amazement, told him she felt exactly the same way. And for some reason, that thrilled him.

Could she *get* this? A love of nature was a big criterion for him in a woman. Except, come to think of it...he'd never brought a woman here before. His friends, yes, and even some camping tours. But never a woman like this.

A woman whose name he didn't know, he reminded himself.

The clouds had rolled closer, bathing the entire river valley in a smoky blue-gray that always soothed his soul. Rain might come, but he knew from experience that it would be no more than a light drizzle, not a storm. That was the kind of rain he loved up here while tucked under the overhang.

Below, the aptly named Snake River wended through it all like a navy-blue ribbon that wrapped the package, calm in parts, then whipped up and white where rocks rose up from the riverbed. Rafters and kayakers were few, but visible, dotting the water.

The bird's-eye view of the whole area showed the dense streets and buildings in town, the warren of residential streets on the east side, and the woods, hills, and forested areas on the west side of the river where he grew up.

"Do you have your bearings?" he asked. "You see Sentinel Bridge right there, with the diner?"

"Oh yes. I do see it."

"And A To Z and, to the right of that, the boathouse I'm not in the middle of renovating with nine days left." Which reminded him why they were up here. For honesty and admissions that he hadn't heard word one of yet.

"Oh, there's an airport here!" She sounded more dismayed than surprised. "I had no idea."

"That's one of the reasons Eagle's Ridge does so well in tourism. And it's the thing that started it all."

"How's that?" she asked.

"When the men who founded the town had the opportunity to buy a lot of this land cheaply after World War II ended, they came up here to survey the possibilities and decide how to divide it all. One of the ideas was an airstrip to make money and attract tourists. It still does, and the commuter flights have really helped build Eagle's Ridge into an easily accessible mountain playground. Now that Ryder Westbrook is the manager, it's going to grow even more."

"Oh. I didn't realize it was so easy to get here." Again, she didn't seem thrilled with that idea.

"Not *that* easy." And why did it bother her?

"What about the eagle?" she asked.

"The one my grandpa saw?" He turned and pointed to an overhang of stone and trees just above them on the side of the mountain. It was his protection from the rain and why the fire pit was below it. "Grandpa told me it was up there. A bald eagle, looking down on all of them."

"That's a wonderful story."

Not as wonderful as the one he was waiting to hear from her.

"It's such a unique story and such a special place. Could I talk to those men? Are they still alive?"

More procrastination. "Oh hell, yeah. Old as these hills, but they love to talk, especially my grandfather and his pal David Bennett."

"I really want to talk to them."

"Jadyn," he said pointedly. "You promised."

She sighed and leaned into him a little as a chilly breeze made her shiver. She had on only a sweater and down vest, and the temperature was probably freezing to her thin tropical blood.

Putting his arm around her, he guided her back around the fire pit.

"Come and sit here."

"Did you make this fire pit?"

"The original was made by my grandpa. He brought me up here when I was young, and I've been camping here for years and always improving the pit, especially after winter." When she sat down on the rocks that faced the pit, he grabbed some of the small kindling he kept tucked away. Throwing it in, he dug through the backpack for a lighter.

"You mean you don't rub two sticks together?"

He gave her a look. "And if you switch subjects, ask another question, or otherwise delay what you came up here to tell me, I'm going to…"

He looked at her, seeing a mix of emotions in her eyes he couldn't quite read. He stared at her for a minute, too long, really, but he couldn't look away.

"Come on, Jadyn," he finally whispered. "Talk to me."

"All right, all right." She blew out a noisy breath and finally nodded. "I'm a very successful interior designer in Miami."

Which he already knew or…thought he knew. "So your résumé was truthful?" He brushed some dirt from his hands over the small fire and sat down next to her, getting close to warm her even more.

"Most of it, yeah. Did you call any references?"

"No. Should I have?"

She swallowed noisily. "I'm not sure the numbers would work, but if they did, you'd probably be talking to an FBI agent."

He inched back at the answer, not sure he'd heard right. "The FBI?"

"I'm not running from a boyfriend or anything like that," she said. "I was in the wrong place at the wrong time, and for my own protection, the FBI sent me away. Off the grid, as they say."

She turned a little, giving him the chance to look

right into her bottomless eyes and decide if this was the truth or not.

He stared back at her, hating that he was leaning to *not*. "Are you serious?"

"Dead. And if I don't want to be, I'm not saying any more than that."

"What? You have to tell me what happened. You know I won't quit asking until I know."

"I'm beginning to figure that out." She pulled her legs up and wrapped her arms around them as if she could ball herself up from what she knew she had to say. "One of my clients, my biggest, wealthiest, most profitable client, I might add, turned out to be a drug trafficker. A Bolivian drug lord, actually, living the high life in a multimillion-dollar penthouse in Miami Beach that I was redesigning for him."

Possible. Plausible, even. He knew quite a bit from the Coast Guard about trafficking and knew that Bolivia, though landlocked, bordered some heavy hitters. Bolivia had been gaining in stature in the South American narcotics trade, and Miami was well known as a hub for US-based transnational drug rings.

But that kind of person seemed like an unlikely client for this woman who demanded a full background and history before picking a paint color. He tamped down his doubts and asked, "Okay, so what happened?"

"I honestly don't know," she said. "One day I was home, in my apartment, minding my own business, and someone knocked on the door, and it was a woman who I thought was one of his many hangers-on. Rich people are surrounded by sycophants, something I've gotten used to in my business. I opened the door, and wham, she flashes a badge, tells me she's undercover FBI and that they'd almost arrested my client the night before."

"But they didn't?" And if they hadn't, would they really tell a civilian? Not a chance. Not a molecule of a chance.

"He got wind of what was going down—I have no idea how, who, or what they were going to do. All I know is someone in his organization told him that he'd been betrayed by a woman."

"The one at your door. The undercover FBI agent."

She nodded and eyed him as if she'd picked up the note of skepticism in his voice. "I'm telling the truth," she said simply.

He didn't answer and saw that register on her face, too. Man, she was easier to read without makeup. Her color rose and fell, and her eyes were less distracting without the paint, and far more honest.

"He decided that woman had to be me, that I was the undercover agent or mole or whatever."

"Why? What would make him think that?"

"I didn't ask at the time because the sense of urgency was real." She rubbed her arms, but not against any chill since the fire warmed them both. He imagined her chill was from the memory of what happened...or knowing she was lying.

Why couldn't he tell?

"This agent literally swooped me out of town," she said. "She packed my bags, drove me to Miami International, stuffed a ticket to Seattle in my hand, and the whole time, she was firing instructions at me, which were basically 'get the hell out of Dodge and fast.' Oh, and don't trust anyone. That was rule number one."

He didn't say a word for a long time, playing this through in his mind.

After a moment, her shoulders fell. "You don't believe me."

"I…I don't not believe you," he said. "But as stories go, this one is out there."

She looked disgusted. "What's 'out there' is a guy who wants me dead. So I followed her rules. When I got to Seattle, I got on a bus that was going as far as I could go while staying in Washington State, which was one of the rules."

"Why?"

She choked. "I don't know, Adam. Maybe proximity to an FBI office?"

"Closest one's in Portland. In Oregon."

"I honestly don't know. I'm just doing what I was told to stay alive." She notched her head in the direction of town. "I had no idea this place has an airport, because that makes it a heck of a lot less appealing to me."

"So you wouldn't have come?" And all this could have been avoided…or missed, depending on his point of view.

"I picked the town by looking at a departures board in a bus station. The name sounded…uplifting."

He didn't say anything, but poked a stick at the fire, still thinking it all through. Why would she just make up a wild-ass story like that if it wasn't true?

Because she was on the run from the law herself? She was involved in a drug ring? Who knew? She did. She knew and wasn't telling him.

"It should all be over in a few weeks, though," she added. "And I can go home."

"Are you sure? How?"

"The agent called me, and they have a new plan to get him. But he still thinks it's me, and he thinks I took something important from his office that's missing, so…"

"What was it?"

"I don't know," she said again, frustration in the words. "I am not in the inner circle of FBI undercover activities, Adam. I was his interior designer one minute and on his hit list the next."

"What's this guy's name?"

She closed her eyes. "I can't tell you names."

"Why? You worried I'll Google him and find out you're lying?"

She flinched a little at that. "I don't know what you'd find if you Googled him, probably the fact that he owns a penthouse on Ocean Avenue worth four million and runs 'multiple companies,' if you found anything at all."

"What were you doing for him?"

"I told you. Renovating and redecorating."

"So if he was a drug lord, why didn't you find that out when you tried to get into his psyche so you could be inspired to do his design?" He heard the note of cynicism in his voice, and judging by the look on her face, she heard it, too. And it hurt.

Damn it.

"He was pretty much throwing money at me."

"Cash?" he asked, still a little too sharply.

She turned away and didn't dignify that one with a response. "I'm not lying," she whispered. "Is that what you think? Really?"

"I don't know what I think," he said softly. "Tell me more about this guy. And the FBI agent."

"Don't you think it's better if you don't know?"

"What if someone by that name comes to town and I find out because I've lived here most of my life and I know everyone? I could warn you if Mr. Bolivian Bad Guy checks into the Broadleaf."

"He won't," she said.

"How do you know?"

She answered with a deep sigh. "I've told you everything I'm comfortable sharing. That's why I didn't want to show ID to the police. What if they put it in some file somewhere and he has access or a cop on the take who gives him the information? I don't know how powerful this guy is."

"Can I see your ID?"

"No."

"Will you tell me your real name?"

"No."

"What would you do if I contacted my friend the policeman and asked him to run a little check on FBI undercover operations on Bolivian drug lords in Miami?"

She turned to him, her eyes surprisingly welling with tears. "What if I'm telling the truth and that gets me killed? How would you feel about that, Adam?"

The question punched him right in the gut. She was right, of course. And one death on a man's soul was enough.

Slowly, he stood and smothered the fire with some dirt. Then he brushed his hands on his jeans and reached for the pack. "We better get down the mountain before it rains."

She squinted up at him, those tears still threatening and torturing him. "Do you believe me?"

Yes. No. Maybe. "I don't know," he answered honestly. "But you're not going to die on my watch, that's for damn sure."

She closed her eyes in relief, and one tear trickled down, slicing through him. "Thank you."

"You can stay at my apartment."

After a moment, she held her hand up to him. "Thanks for the rescue, Coastie."

He lifted her easily and pulled her up to his chest. When she looked up at him, the impact of her dark eyes and sweet, vulnerable face damn near buckled his knees. They held each other's gaze, like a silent promise, and then she closed her eyes, and he had to fight with everything he had not to kiss her.

Because that was the last damn thing he needed.

Chapter Nine

Adam's apartment above A To Z Watersports was small, not quite a studio, but not quite a legitimate one-bedroom, either. And as apartments go, it was dull. Except for the view from every window, the open space had very little life in it.

Curious, since he seemed to have so much. At least, he did when he was outdoors.

The bed was wedged into an alcove barely big enough for a queen-size mattress, but it was under a huge window that faced the river and mountains. The living area was furnished with a couple of recliners and a love seat, adjacent to a kitchen with a small table, two chairs, and a single counter top.

With the exceptions of a few Coast Guard certificates, the space had a distinctly temporary feel.

"How long have you been here?" she asked after getting the tour that took less than a minute.

"Two years. Little more, actually." As if he picked up on her assessment, he nodded. "I thought it would be short-term, but I put every dime into the boathouse, so Zane lets me live here basically for the cost of utilities. After I bought the boathouse from my grandfather, I'm sinking my entire savings into the renovation."

"Oh." She slipped into a chair at the kitchen table and reached into her bag for the drawings. "Then you want to see my ideas?"

"You're kidding, right?" He joined her at the table. "Pretty sure I've been wanting to do that all day. Longer."

She spread the papers out, trying to put them in some kind of order, but he snagged the first one, flipping it around to face him.

"That's the loft?"

"Yes, that's the loft, and while we were hiking, I was thinking the design of the stairs could somehow emulate the mountain. But, of course, these are really rough sketches for color, not voice."

He looked up. "Voice? The boathouse has a voice?"

"All spaces have something to say. It's my job to bring that voice to life."

He grunted under his breath. "I honestly don't want it to be that elaborate."

"But the rooms have to say something to the people in them."

"How about 'welcome, keep it clean, and go to bed because we put in to raft at seven a.m.'?"

She smiled and shook her head. "You have a huge opportunity here to make the living quarters as exciting as the adventures. This town is special, and you have to know that. It's beautiful and has a unique history. And the founders are still alive! They should be part of it."

He didn't answer as he studied a few more sketches.

"I'd like to put a mural on the wall there," Jane said, her own voice rising with excitement. "I just sketched the mountains, but I want something more...historic. The geography is out the window and will be reflected in the earth tones and some simple but exciting touches, like the stairs. But the history has to be there, too. Any ideas? Did your grandfather share the history with you?"

"Sure," he said, flipping to another page. "The history of how he got drunk and bet the good land, and John Westbrook cheated or stole his girl or...*something*. It was damn near seventy years ago, and not one of those old Army Air Corps coots actually remembers the details. Just that they had to hate each other."

"I don't want to capture some ancient feud." No, that was the opposite of what she wanted.

"Of course not." He looked at the kitchen design. "This is nice, Jadyn. I love the greens and browns and that sort of smattering of yellow there, if it doesn't take too much time to paint."

"It's called a pop of color, and it's supposed to capture those yellow flowers on the side of the mountain." She rested her chin in her hand. "But what about the ridge? What about the eagle? That would make a great mural."

"I guess." He sounded far from convinced. "I don't want to hurt your feelings or silence the, uh, *voice* of this place, but I don't have time to commission a mural. We need to get the appliances in, finish the bathroom, and maybe paint the walls. The stairs have to be to code, too, so I'm not all hyped about something that *emulates* the mountain."

He could barely hide his utter lack of enthusiasm for her plan.

"I'm hoping to finish the hard-core carpentry this weekend when my buddy Ford's in town, although..." He exhaled. "It's not a penthouse with a massive budget and all the time in the world, Jadyn. It's just a dormitory for kids."

"A dormitory for kids who are in trouble, at risk, or

living in bad situations," she added. "That's what you said."

"Kids who need to straighten up and fly right."

"Exactly." She snapped her fingers and pointed at him. "I bet someone who was a member of the Army Air Corps would have a lot to contribute to that concept."

"I'm sure they do, but—"

"Straighten up and fly right," she repeated, dragging out the words as they sank into her head. "Oh yes! That can be the theme of the whole thing. That's the voice, the message. The military influence here in this gorgeous slice of rugged land!" She clasped her hands together as the vision got more clear with every second. "Oh, I love it!"

"I…guess. Except, all I want are beds and a living area."

"Kind of like this lovely apartment of yours?"

He gave a quick, self-deprecating laugh. "I told you, I thought it was temporary. I know it's boring."

"Boredom is why a lot of these kids are in trouble, Adam."

"No, they're in trouble because they smoke weed and get drunk and do stupid stuff."

"Like gluing pennies to locks?"

"We weren't drunk or high, just…kids."

"Because you had direction and family and history and this beautiful town behind you. Am I right?"

"I guess, but…" He considered that, nodding slowly. "Yeah, you're right. That's exactly what…yeah, you're right."

"What were you going to say?" she asked.

"Nothing, not important. You totally get what I want to do for these kids."

"Why?"

He frowned as if the question confused him. "I don't know, but I do want them to straighten up and fly right, so if you're hell-bent on a theme, yeah. But only if it can be done in time. The corporate tour arrives a week from Friday."

She looked hard at him, studying his face the way he'd looked at her when she told him her story up on the mountain. Like there had to be more to this and she was trying to read it in his expression. "I meant why is it so important to you?" she asked.

He shrugged, maybe a little too casually and quickly, giving the question no thought at all. "Because I want to give them this." He gestured toward the window and view beyond. "I want them to appreciate the beauty and power of nature, that's all."

Was it? "It's personal, right?"

After a moment, he said, "It's important to me, and you don't need to dig any deeper than that. Stick with this geography and history, okay?"

He'd helped her out of a jam today, and then he'd been kind enough to back off when she wanted him to, so she nodded in agreement.

"We'll give them all of that and more," she assured him. "During the day, while they hike and raft. But at night, in that cavern of a boathouse, let them soak up the fact that these four men, comrades-in-arms, took this little piece of paradise and made it this amazing place with families and diners and thriving businesses."

"Comrades-in-arms?" He chuckled. "That's rich. Well, maybe at first. Then they started fighting over land and split into two sides, which were essentially rich against poor, and put a rift in this town deeper than that river."

"But that's part of the history," she argued. "And you said it was over."

"It'll be over when they die, which, with all of them in their nineties, won't be long."

"That makes it even more important that we do it now. I bet they have so much stuff we could use. Memorabilia, pictures, keepsakes and newspaper articles and medals. Does your grandpa have that?"

He winced. "Might be a sore spot. He lost almost everything but his life in a flood last month. Right now, he's living with my dad and damned upset about it."

"In his nineties? I wouldn't think that would upset him."

"He's very independent, or at least, he was."

She considered that. "Then he can work on the project with us. Can we get them together?"

"All in one place?" He blew out a breath. "The feud might be technically over, but I doubt John Westbrook's going to hang with those guys. But..." He angled his head and smiled. "It's Wednesday, right?"

"All day."

He looked down at his chunky sports watch. "In forty-five minutes, two of them will be at No Man's Land. Grandpa Max and his best friend, David Bennett, go every Wednesday for the WarBird Special at 4:45, rain or shine."

She grinned and looked out at the drizzle that had finally started to dampen the town. "Perfect. We'll meet them there."

He rolled his eyes. "Of course we will."

What the hell was wrong with him? The question burned in Adam's brain as they walked silently to No Man's Land. Next to him, Jadyn tucked into a jacket he'd found in the rental room downstairs. She literally had come to Washington State without any outerwear at all. So, that much of her story rang true.

The rain was light, but steady, with steel-gray skies and a hint of winter clinging stubbornly to the April air.

He sneaked a glance at the woman beside him. She wanted to give the boathouse a voice. What the hell? And he still didn't even know her real name, which irked him.

And yet, here he was, taking her to No Man's Land so she could interview Grandpa Max and David Bennett.

"I got it," he murmured, reaching for the handle of the large glass door to hold it open for her, peering through to the dining room. It wasn't crowded at the luncheon bar, but the booths were pretty full with the early crowd.

As they walked in, he dipped to see into the kitchen and spied his father behind the pass, hard at work. No surprise there. He took a lot of nights off, but never Wednesday. He'd worked the WarBird Special every Wednesday since Adam was a kid.

And Grandpa was in his usual booth, eating grilled cheese with bacon, with his best friend across from him, dipping toast in coffee because half his teeth were gone. The two of them were talking politics and old movies, and reminiscing. Loudly.

"They're over there," Adam said, gesturing to the corner. None of the tables nearby was taken, but if they had been, Adam would have known those patrons were tourists. The locals knew Max had to holler for David to hear him and David answered in kind.

"Just follow the yelling," Adam said, nudging her in the right direction.

"That's the thing, David. You can't just rebuild the

same house! It's never the same! It's..." He turned to see Adam coming closer, his whole wrinkly face spreading into a wide smile. "There's my grandson!"

"Who is handsome?" David asked.

But Max ignored him, his old gaze landing on Jadyn. His blue eyes had dimmed over his many years, but the man could still give a piercing stare when he wanted to. And by the way he was locked on her, he wanted to.

"Oh, no, don't get up," Jadyn murmured as they reached the table.

"Can't stop him," Adam said. Almost a hundred years of life, ingrained military protocol, and basic manners dictated that Max Tucker stand when a woman came into his presence.

He smoothed the five strands of gray hair he had left and grinned with yellowed teeth in admiration. "And who is this beautiful angel?"

Jadyn laughed and self-consciously brushed some hair off her face. Was it possible she really didn't think she was beautiful with or without makeup? Adam found that hard to believe, but stepped in to do the introductions.

"Grandpa, this is Jadyn McAllister, a designer I've hired to help me finish the boathouse. Jadyn, this is Max Tucker and David Bennett."

"Jadyn?" Max repeated, frowning, then turning to David. "It's Adam's new..." He hesitated and looked at Adam. "He'll never hear that design business," he said under his breath. "Adam's new girlfriend," he announced loudly. "Jadyn."

"Jane?" David put his toast down and furrowed bushy gray brows.

"Jadyn," Adam corrected. "Like the stone with an n."

"Jadyn," Grandpa said. "Pretty." He looked her up and down, nodding. "So pretty."

"She wants to ask you guys some questions about town history," Adam explained. "Would you mind?"

"Mind?" The old man almost chortled with glee. "Nobody ever wants to listen to us talk about that."

"Talk about what?" David insisted, leaning forward and putting a hand behind a giant teacup of an ear that had apparently earned him the handle Dumbo in his military days.

"History," Jadyn supplied, speaking loud and clear.

"A mystery?" David yelled. "I love a good mystery."

Adam resisted rolling his eyes, Jadyn just smiled, but Grandpa threw a look at his friend. "Why in the name of all that's holy don't you wear that hearing aid?"

David flicked his hand at the suggestion. "My ears are just fine if you'll speak up."

Grandpa gestured for Jadyn to take a seat. "Right here, young lady. Next to me."

"No, next to me, Jane," David bellowed, patting the leather seat.

Without correcting him, she slipped into the booth, and Grandpa tapped Adam's arm. "Go get her a Coke. Or talk to your dad. We don't need you. Leave us with this delightful creature."

"You okay with that?" Adam asked her, a little relieved not to have to sit and hear David yell for however long this would take. "You want anything to drink?"

"Sure." She smiled up at him. "Ice water is fine."

He nodded and gave a slight salute to his grandfather. "Keep an eye on her."

"Oh, I will," he assured him. "Both eyes, but no hands."

Chuckling at the old man, Adam headed behind the bar, nodding to the new night-shift waitress, Mandy, which surprised him, because Brenda, like Dad, always covered Wednesday nights. So now she'd missed Monday morning and Wednesday night. Odd.

But Mandy seemed a little distracted as she looked at her pad and tried to fill a soda at the same time, so he decided not to ask her to get Jadyn's water now.

"Hey, Dad," he said, coming around the back to see what was on the grill and stove. "How's it going?"

He shot a frown up, then glanced at the pass before lowering his voice. "She's real sweet, that Mandy, but she's screwed up a few orders tonight."

"Where's Brenda?" Adam asked.

"She worked all day." He flipped a burger with a little more force than necessary. "And tonight the people in that photography class are getting together to preview the materials and share pictures and *talk*." He damn near spat the last word.

"Well, she has to have a life," he said, echoing Bailey and remembered his siblings' conjecture about Dad and…no. Not possible. Not within the realm of possible. "I'm sure Mandy'll be fine, and the place isn't even that crowded."

"She *has* a life," he said, as if Adam hadn't even spoken. "I mean, this place is full of her friends who come in here, and she has…" His hand froze as he picked up a pan of sizzling onions. "It's not a bad life," he muttered. "Even if some people think it is."

Adam knew exactly who Dad meant. An age-old, familiar, and entirely unwelcome resentment coiled in Adam's chest. After what? Seventeen years? You'd think he'd have let go of that feeling of wanting to punch a wall when he thought about Mom leaving.

"It's fine," Adam said quickly. "It's a good place to work and…live."

"Except when it's not."

Adam frowned. "Something wrong, Dad?"

"No, no. Nothing. What are you doing here, anyway? Trying to lose that bet with Zane?"

"Yeah, basically." Adam leaned against the counter, staying out of his father's way while the older man went through the motions of preparing seven different dinners, all in various stages of readiness. "I brought Jadyn, the designer. She's talking to Grandpa and David about the town history."

Dad shot him a look. "Why?"

"She thinks it should be incorporated in the decoration of the boathouse quarters." Give it a *voice*, which was too out-there to share with Dad when he was concentrating on finishing a burger platter. He put the plate on the pass, rang the bell, and sighed when nothing happened in twenty seconds.

"Brenda would have that steaming hot and in front of the customer by now."

"Want me to take it?"

"I'm here, I'm here." Mandy sailed up to the pass, looking frazzled. She reached for the burger, frowned, and then looked at Dad. "It was a cheeseburger. Did I not write that? Sorry!"

Dad blew out a breath but kept his cool, nodding to her and grabbing a stack of American cheese slices. "Gimme a sec."

When Mandy disappeared, he put the burger back on the grill and shot a look to Adam. "Brenda would never have made that mistake."

"And that's why you're a little ticked off that she's not here."

"I told you she worked a whole day shift." Dad pressed the meat to help melt the cheese. Pressed hard.

"So it's fine that..." His words trailed off as he replated the burger and glanced at the ticket. "And, yes, would you take this out to table five before they leave and never come back?"

"Sure." He grabbed the platter, but felt his father's eyes on him. "I got this, Dad. I've waited tables in this place before." Didn't like it, but he did it.

"Lemme ask you something, Adam."

He nodded, waiting.

"Why are you on some wild-goose history chase when all you wanted was someone to help you buy stuff for that boathouse project and your kids camp?"

He stared at his father, unable to answer that.

"'Cause of her, right?"

"I guess so."

Dad nodded as if Adam had confirmed something that wasn't even part of this conversation. "Women. You can't live with 'em and you can't..."

"Send 'em down river?" Adam joked.

"Not what I was thinking. Come on, get that food out."

He almost bumped into Mandy on the way out, and she sheepishly took the burger to deliver it. Adam grabbed an ice water from behind the luncheon counter and headed back to the corner booth, where the three of them were in deep, and loud, conversation.

"And you have to hear this," Grandpa added.

Jadyn was tapping notes into her phone.

"Listen to me, Jane," Grandpa insisted.

She looked up. "I am, I promise. It's just that I don't want to forget anything. This is amazing!"

Adam slowed his step, taking in the exchange. Had she decided it wasn't worth correcting them about her name or...or...was he imagining that instant, natural response to the wrong name?

"There are helmets!" Grandpa announced. "You have the helmets, right, David?"

"I gave 'em to Hildie Fontana. Leather for the fighters and a fifty-mission crush garrison cap. Course I kept that one."

"What is a fifty-mission crush?" Jadyn asked, a little breathless.

David grinned, clearly having no hearing problems when he was talking about the old days with a willing and beautiful audience. He cleared his throat and leaned forward.

"Bombers wear garrison caps, Janie. They're shaped different and kind of stick out here." He patted the sides of his head. "But the bomber puts his headset over the hat, and every time he wears it, the puffy sides get a little more crushed. You want to know how tough a man was? Take a look at his crush. Fifty-mission crush." His wrinkled mouth turned down as he nodded at how impressive that was. "The best."

"You have a hat like this? Were you a bomber?" She asked the question loud and clear, and David shook his head.

"I was a mechanic. Crew chief, if you must know. The bomber was Rusty McCoy, and he loved my work. Died about twenty years ago, and his wife sent his cap to me. Said Rusty told her it was my work that got him home after every mission." He beamed with pride. "You bet I have that cap. I even have—"

"Jane," Grandpa interrupted.

She whipped around to face him. "What?"

"I have another idea for you."

Adam just stared, processing, wondering.

"You do need to go talk to Hildie Fontana," Grandpa said.

"Oh yeah," David agreed. "She's got a garage full of stuff she hauls out every year for Founder's Day."

"Founders' *weekend*," Grandpa corrected with a sniff. "The 'day' is just for that egomaniac Westbrook. The *weekend* is for all four of us, so that makes it the real holiday."

"Oh, for crying out loud," Adam interjected, sliding in next to David. "This is really getting far afield," he said to Jadyn. "We still need a *sink* in that place. Not helmets hanging on the wall."

She ignored him, tapping on her phone. "Hildie Fontana, you said? Adam, do you know how I can find her?"

"Stand in the middle of town and sniff for gossip," he said.

"No gossip, just history." She flashed her smile at him, which was even brighter than when they'd started this madness. "And wait till you hear this story they told me."

"I've heard all the stories," he assured her.

"Well, I didn't hear half of it," David joked, sipping his coffee. "Did I, Janie?"

"Janie?" Adam asked, lifting a brow.

Her cheeks paled slightly, which he might never have noticed if she'd been wearing rouge or blush, or whatever they called it. But he could see it now.

"What's important is that I have been inspired beyond belief," she said, glancing at the notes on her phone. "Do you know about Sleepy Time Gal, Adam?"

"The B-26 Marauder?" Did he know about the plane Captain Max Tucker flew in the war? "Uh, yeah. I've heard of it. Seen the yawning pinup girl that was painted on the side."

Grandpa hooted. "What a woman."

"She sounds wonderful!" Jadyn was undeterred in her enthusiasm. "We have to do something with mugs."

"Mugs?" Adam asked. Maybe she meant rugs. Maybe his hearing was as bad as David's because—

"Squadron mugs!" David supplied, hearing every damn word. "Janie had a great idea for those."

"*Janie* did?" Adam didn't know whether to laugh, pull his hair out, or ask her the question that had started burning in his brain.

"It's just easier," she whispered, "than, you know, correcting them."

Was it? Or was it—

"Would you guys consider joining the other two founders for a special presentation when we finish?" she asked. "A dedication, of sorts?"

David and Grandpa looked at each other. "Possibly," Grandpa said.

Adam slowly pushed up from the booth, trying not to explode in frustration. "Well, I guess if you're planning a dedication, you're planning to be finished in a little more than a week. Right...*Janie*?"

She shot him a narrow-eyed glare. "Absolutely."

"Then you better get to work, young lady," Grandpa said. "This is the first thing I've been excited about since..." He looked up at Adam. "Since before that damn flood."

Jadyn gave a smile to Grandpa, reaching over the table to squeeze his gnarled old hand. "You've been a huge help, Max. And you, too, David." She put her other hand on David's skinny shoulder and patted it. "I'm so happy for this."

"What? You want a kiss?" he yelled back, making her laugh.

David joined her and looked up at Adam. "She's a

keeper, this Jane. Good thing she likes you and not your brother."

"Why's that?" Not that he was sure he wanted to hear.

"'Cause then they'd be Zane and Jane!" David hooted, and Grandpa joined in with a guffaw that turned into a cough. But Jadyn just smiled, her expression giving nothing away, and made no attempt to correct them.

"Thank you for everything," she finally said, pushing out of the booth. "I'll be in touch, I promise!"

She waved her goodbye and let Adam lead her to the door, a bounce in her step that he hadn't seen before.

He pulled open the heavy door and held it for her again, letting her get a few steps ahead. Then he took a breath and called out, "Jane, I have an idea."

She turned around. "What is it?"

For a long moment, neither one said a word. He just watched her shoulders sink as she realized her mistake. "Why don't you tell me your real name?"

"I think you already know it."

Chapter Ten

"**J**ane."

From the sofa in his apartment, Jane looked over the wineglass that Adam had just handed her and met his gaze. "That's what they call me."

He sat next to her, picking up a green beer bottle and twisting the top off, holding it up to her for a toast. "Here's to progress. I finally know your name." He took a drink, then lowered the bottle. "Jane." It had to be the tenth time he'd said it since they came back from the restaurant. "I like it."

She gave a shaky smile and sipped, the deep tones of the Cabernet warming in her mouth. "It's better than Jadyn," she agreed. "But that's what the FBI agent told me to use and I'm scared not to, in case some other agent has to come and find me and that's all he or she has to go on."

"Not sure it works that way, but I think Jane is a great name. Solid. Sexy. Smart." He eyed her with just enough heat to make her nerve endings singe. "It suits you."

"It suits this." She gestured toward her unadorned face. "Plain Jane."

He sighed, took one more sip, then leaned back and put his arm along the back of the sofa, his fingertips just grazing her shoulder. "I find it impossible to believe you don't know how beautiful you are."

She fought the urge to look skyward, not wanting to seem like she was begging for compliments. And certainly not wanting to hand him a shovel and say, *Here, dig deep and find out all that's wrong with me.*

Once she walked out of her last home the day she turned eighteen, she never told a soul about her childhood. It wasn't relevant. It was ancient, dark history that never needed to be brought out into the light and examined. Her new world was better, the best she could make it.

Yes, that meant she didn't get close to people, but so be it.

"It shouldn't take you quite so long to say thank you," Adam said. When she blinked at him, pulling herself back to the moment, he added, "When someone calls you beautiful."

"Thank you," she said softly, angling the glass to slide the wine from side to side. "Let's talk about the boathouse. I got a zillion ideas from those men."

He scanned her face, not answering.

"Maybe you could give the kids a souvenir—like a mug or a cap—if they complete a number of 'adventure' missions. Wouldn't that be cool?"

"Actually, yes. But we're not done talking about you."

"Oh yes, we are. You know all you need to know, and don't even think about asking my last name."

"But what should I call you?"

She dug for humor. "Anything but late for dinner?"

"Jane or Jadyn?"

"Stick with Jadyn. It's safer now that people know me as that."

"Not David Bennett."

She laughed. "They're great guys, honestly. How lucky you are to have such a character for a grandfather."

"What are your grandfathers like?"

She took another sip, delaying the response, then thought of another. "Do you think a mural of the plane with the pinup girl would be appropriate for kids?"

"Were you born in Miami?" he asked.

Her eyes shuttered closed. "You won't quit, will you?"

"Never. They called me Tenacious Tuck in the Coast Guard, and any of my family or friends will tell you the word quitting is not in my dictionary." He looked down for a moment, as if a thought had taken hold, then took a slug of beer.

"I noticed your impatience."

"It's not impatience, it's just focus. Determination. Tenacity, yes."

"When did you discover that?" she asked, happy he'd just handed her a subject change.

He gave a hearty laugh. "Your ability to deflect a personal question is absolutely masterful."

"Thank you." She added a smile, which was easy while sitting this close to him and hearing him laugh. "When did you discover you were Tenacious Tuck?"

"Okay, okay. You win. Let's see." He dropped his head back, maybe not aware that his fingers had settled on her hair, very lightly threading it as he thought. But Jane was aware. Far too aware of the tiny sparks of attraction and tension flicking all over her body. Very aware that they were close, touching, and sharing secrets.

All too aware of how good that felt.

"I was the oldest, you know," he said.

"You're a twin."

"Born first by four minutes. Name starts with an A, while the other one got a Z."

"What's the deal with that, anyway?" she asked. "Any special meaning? The beginning and the end? The first and the last?"

"The whack job who is my mother?" he suggested.

"Is she really that bad?" Because, as whack job mothers went, nobody could touch Susan McAllen.

"Yeah," he said simply. "I mean, I told you she chose a fake family over a real one. She picked fame and fortune over a simple life with a man who loved her. She gave up on us. So I guess the answer to your question about when my tenacity issues started? Probably the day she walked out with promises she never kept and a little too big of a smile on her face."

Jane's heart cracked a little, the impact of his words hitting home hard enough for her to set the wineglass down so it didn't slip out of her hand. "I understand that."

He whipped his head around to face her, his eyes flashing like gas flames of hot blue. "You're defending her?"

"No, actually, I was saying I understand how that could gut you."

His expression softened. "It did, I won't lie. Still does, at times."

"Do you talk to her?"

"As little as possible. Bailey does, I think, although she doesn't share it with me."

"How does Zane feel about her?"

"About like I do, I guess. We don't discuss her. Ever. And she's remarried to some rich dude with grown kids, and they travel and live the life." His fingers tangled a little tighter in her hair. "It's not important."

"I'd say something like that is very important," she replied, reaching for her wine. She took a sip and leaned back, and his hand went right back to her hair. Somehow, it was natural and comforting. And irresistible.

"You still haven't told me a thing about your childhood," he said. "*Your* mother. Your life. None of that would go against the FBI rules, would it?"

"No," she answered simply.

"Jadyn..." He shook his head like he was shaking off the name. "*Jane*. I want to know."

"I know you do, but why? I'm doing a job for you and leaving when it's safe. You don't need to know anything about me."

A little anguish pulled his brows together as he threaded her hair and stroked her neck. Could he feel the goose bumps that was causing?

"But I want to. I want to hear your story and know what makes you tick." He inched a little closer, holding her gaze with one that was so heated and intense she felt it burn right through her.

"Why does it matter?" she asked again.

"Because I have this little rule. Archaic, maybe. Old-school. But I like to know something about a woman before I..." He didn't finish, and she didn't breathe.

"Before you kiss me?"

"That's where I'm going." He closed the space but didn't kiss her, and Jane felt her whole being slip a little. Dangerous slope, this one, but so, so tempting.

"You really want to complicate things, don't you?" she whispered.

"No. I really want to kiss you."

She didn't answer but felt her eyes shutter closed as his lips lightly brushed hers, shocking her with the initial touch of his mouth. His lips were smooth, surprisingly so, but whiskers rubbed her chin and upper lip, the sensation so intense a whimper escaped her throat.

He took that as a sound of pleasure, she guessed, as he held her face tenderly in his hands, angling her head a bit, deepening the kiss. He broke it reluctantly, then pressed his lips against her cheeks and jaw and gave the softest, sexiest moan that came from deep in his chest.

"What happened to the rule?"

"Tell me your last name, and we'll call it"—he trailed some kisses over her throat and went back to her lips—"covered." And he did just that, covering her mouth and opening his lips.

"No." She eased back.

"No, don't kiss you, or no to the last name?"

She wanted to say both. She should say both. "No to the last name."

"So you have no problem kissing?"

Looking at him for a long time, she stroked his cheek with one finger, loving the roughness of those burnished-gold whiskers. "I have plenty of problems, but kissing you isn't one of them."

He didn't answer, but still stared into her eyes. "How about where you were born?"

"No."

"Siblings?"

"No."

"College?"

"No."

He shut his eyes. "You're making me go against my kissing principles, because I don't want you to be a stranger."

"That kiss wasn't strange. It was—" She jerked back and looked around after a soft digital ring she rarely heard sounded in the room. "That's my phone." She was up instantly, looking for her bag, which she'd left by the front door.

Lydia. It had to be Lydia. Darting to the bag, she yanked open the side pocket, but her fingers fumbled a little. "I can't miss this call," she said, more to herself than to him. Finally, she snagged the phone, tapped it, and pressed it to her ear, only at that moment realizing he'd hear everything she'd say. "Yes, hello?"

But the line was dead, or silent.

"Hello? Hello? Lydia?"

Nothing.

"Oh!" She fisted her hand and grunted as frustration whipped through her. "It only rang twice. How could that happen?" She looked at the phone, which was painfully simple and certainly not "smart." There was no number, and the display just said Unknown Caller. Still, she could hit Call Back.

"I'm going to try and call," she said to Adam. "Could I have some privacy, please?"

He blew out a breath. "Who's Lydia?"

She gave him a look she hoped he'd understand.

"That would be another 'no,'" he said, proving he most certainly did read her non-verbals. "Jane, this is *my* 'no'—no, you can't do this."

"Do what? I didn't kiss you, Adam. You kissed me."

"You can't take my help in bailing you out of a possible run-in with the police, tell me just enough for me to not know if you're really in danger or yanking my chain for fun, and then send me out of the room for privacy."

"Yanking your chain *for fun*?" She choked the last two words. "Are you kidding me? You think this is fun for me? Lying to people, looking over my shoulder, living in the dark, waiting for a call from an undercover

FBI agent, and then when it comes, she hangs up on me? It's not fun. Designing your boathouse is fun. Kissing you on the sofa is fun. Lying is not fun."

"Okay, okay." He held his hands up as if the fury of the speech had finally gotten through to him. "It's just that you need help. And I want to help you."

"I thought you wanted to know me."

He shrugged, taking a step closer, reaching out a conciliatory hand. "That's part of helping you."

For a moment, she almost cracked. Almost stepped into his arms, pressed her body against his chest, and let it all out. Her ugly past, her name, her life, and the fresh, hot need in her body to take comfort from him.

But that wouldn't be fair to him. It would make a not-so-great situation worse. And that's not what Jane McAllen did. She made things better. The best they could be.

Very slowly, she shook her head and one more time uttered the word he didn't want to hear. "No."

She saw the steel curtain drop over his expression, his blue-green eyes glinting with a mix of anger and challenge. "Fine."

"Is it?"

"It'll have to be." He backed away. "I'm going to take a sleeping bag to the boathouse so you can stay here. Eat, drink, talk on the phone all night if you want, okay?"

No, it wasn't okay. She didn't want to be alone, but she didn't want to let anyone get that close, either. "Sure. That's great."

"If you need anything, just call. I'll give you my cell."

"Okay."

He was gone in a few minutes, leaving Jane to sit on

the sofa and hit redial. Over and over again, until she finally gave up when no one answered.

After a while, she lay down on the bed and tried to imagine what she would add to the décor to make this apartment the best it could be.

But, really, the only thing missing was the man who lived here.

As Adam walked to the boathouse, doubt pricked at him, making the low-grade frustration that burned even worse. That wasn't the only thing burning, either. The achiness that had started low in his belly early in the day only grew worse the more time he spent with her. Jadyn—shit, *Jane*—was not merely beautiful.

That combination of tough and vulnerable wrapped around his chest and magnetically drew him closer. Made him want to help her. Made him want to believe her. Made him want to kiss the hell out of her and so much more.

But…that call.

Adam fished his phone from his pocket and checked the time, doing a quick calculation. It was a little past midnight in DC, not too terribly late to call an old friend. Of course, the chances that Noah Coleman was home were slim. More likely, the badass Navy SEAL was up to his eyeballs with underwater explosives or detonating devices that would crumble a mountain but save a village.

Or so Adam thought, because anytime he asked Noah what he did, the only response was a silent headshake that meant *classified*.

But every once in a while, Noah was at his crash pad in DC, one he shared with an FBI agent.

It was worth a try. Once inside the boathouse, he tapped the contacts and called, smiling when the phone clicked and he heard a familiar voice.

"Adam Ant," Noah said with a tease in his voice. "You drunk-dialing me, honey?"

Adam laughed. "Not quite that desperate, yet. How ya doin', Noah?"

"Alive. Always." He cleared his throat, and Adam could've done a 3-2-1 countdown to the subject change. "What's happening in Eagle's Ridge? You get that stupid boathouse finished yet?"

"Working on it." Slowly. "But I have a favor to ask."

"Not a chance I'm coming back to help you, too." He added a good-natured laugh.

"You talked to Ford," he guessed. He knew that Ford was in DC frequently enough that the two of them threw back beers on a regular basis.

"Yeah. He said you're in way over your head with hammers and nails."

"I might be in over my head, but not with the tools." He threw a glance in the direction of the boathouse door, half worrying she might walk in. Half hoping, too. "No, I have a different kind of favor, which you can feel free to ignore."

"Got me curious. What's up?"

"Didn't you say you share that apartment with a guy who's pretty high up in the FBI?"

"Yeah. Kenny Murphy's a maverick adept in the art of favors, and with supervisory special agent on his badge, he gets shit done. What do you need?"

A lot more than he should be asking for, but Adam went for it anyway. "I need to know if, hypothetically speaking, an undercover operative would take a third party employed by the target but not criminally involved and move that third party out of the picture and tell them to stay off the grid."

Noah was silent for a minute. "So, let me understand, *hypothetically*." He slathered enough sarcasm on the word that they both knew nothing was hypothetical. "Undercover op. What? Drugs? Money laundering? White collar? What kind of hypothetical operation is this?"

"Drugs. FBI infiltrated a large drug ring."

"Well, if that person is an asset that can help the operative, it doesn't seem logical that they would."

"She's not." At least, she'd said she wasn't. "She says she was in the wrong place at the wrong time and got on the wrong radar, and they're protecting her."

"Yeah, they'd do that, I think. It's not officially witness protection. Kind of surprised they'd send her to Eagle's Ridge, but who knows?"

"They sent her to Seattle and told her to basically get lost. She came here on her own."

Noah was quiet, thinking about that. "I'd definitely run that one by Kenny. Can you be a little more specific? He'll dig, but he has to know what for and where."

Adam huffed out a breath. She hadn't really told him anything but her first name and a thin story. Should he break that fragile bit of trust, or just believe her straight out and let it go?

"Trust him," Noah added. "Because you trust me."

"I don't know much," Adam said. "But there's an alleged undercover operation in Miami targeting a Bolivian drug dealer, and the agent is named Lydia, or that's her undercover name. I think."

"No last name?" Noah snorted. "Lots to go on, dude."

"I know, I know. But this woman..."

"Yeah, woman. I got *that* much."

"I hired her to help me design the boathouse. Decorate it, you know?"

"Decorating is out of my area of expertise," he joked.

"Mine, too, which is why I hired her. But she's got this story that the FBI 'whisked' her out of Miami because this baddie wants her dead. Simple question, really. Is that something they'd do?"

"I'll find out," Noah said. "We have an agent's name, a type of crime, US location, and country of origin. That's enough to get started."

"Good," Adam said.

"How about this hypothetical woman?" he teased. "She have a name?"

"Several, but I'd rather not say. I'm already overstepping my bounds."

"You want to help her or not?"

"I want to *believe* her," Adam admitted.

"And you want to help her. I know you, Adam Ant. If there's a rescue in sight, you gotta make it."

He gave a soft laugh at how well his friend knew him. "Jane. Her name's Jane. She's going by the name Jadyn McAllister." He gritted his teeth at what felt like a betrayal of her trust, but if she wasn't going to tell him everything, he damn well was going to do his best to find out. And help her. "Anything you can find out, and keep it on the DL."

"You got it, man."

"Thanks. When are you coming back to Eagle's Ridge?"

"Pffft. Never. Okay, maybe to see Lainey," he said, referring to a local nurse who'd been like a sister to Noah as long as Adam had known him. "But permanently? Not happening. I could no sooner live a normal life in a small town than I could give up my SEAL team with a casual adios. What would I do? You all have something there, and me?" Noah chuckled. "Maybe the Ridgeview Community College TV station needs a tell-it-like-it-is military analyst to report between the cherry pie bake-offs and the latest change in tourist tax."

Adam laughed. "Yeah, you'd suffocate here."

"No shit."

"Not enough white water in the state of Washington to meet your adrenaline needs."

"You know it, bro."

They talked for a few more minutes before hanging up. He couldn't even think about sleeping, so he dragged out the tools and went to work on the bunk beds, getting one finished not too long after midnight.

So he wasn't *that* in over his head. Not with construction, anyway. Jane-not-Jadyn was a whole 'nother story.

Chapter Eleven

"Adam?" Jane tapped on the boathouse door at eight a.m., ready to start the day. She'd slept remarkably well after crawling under the covers of Adam's bed and had awakened with a plan to head straight to the woman named Hildie who kept all the town memorabilia. "Are you awake?"

After a moment, he opened the door and stared down at her with sleepy, sexy blue eyes. His sun-tipped hair was tousled, and scruff the color of whiskey had grown on his cheeks and jaw overnight. He wore…little. She stole a look at the cuts and slopes of a magnificent chest and the gorgeous symmetry of well-defined abs. The boxers hung low, showing more muscles, veins, and a golden-brown trail of hair.

She looked up, trying to swallow. "Good morning."

"What time is it?" he asked, blinking as if the cloudy skies were shining a klieg light on him.

"Time to visit Hildie Fontana. Can you take me to her?" She slipped by him to enter, trying to ignore how warm his skin was when they brushed. Then her eyes fell on the bunk bed in the middle of the room, made of black metal rails that looked exactly like…like something from a jail cell. "Oh, Adam. It's hideous."

He muttered what sounded like a really dark curse, marching around her and stabbing his fingers in his hair and drawing it back, which only made it messier. "Thank you."

"No, I'm sorry, but what were you thinking? Black? Iron? Do they all get orange jumpsuits for pajamas?"

"It was on sale and in stock, and you weren't there to help pick something that *sang* to me to make sure the loft has a *voice*."

She smiled at the tease and went to the bed, running her hand over the rails. "Can you return it?"

He came right up to her, bare chest, boxers and all. "Are you out of your mind? It took me five hours to assemble the thing. The instructions were in Chinese."

"You should have called me," she said, fighting the urge to let her gaze drop over his chiseled torso for another leisurely look.

"You read Chinese?"

"I would never have let you assemble this. And I would have..." She lost the battle and looked. "Yeah, okay." She stepped back and turned to the bed. "I don't know what I'll do with that, I mean, this."

When he didn't answer, she glanced at him, catching the sly smile. "So how'd you sleep...Jane?"

She narrowed her eyes. "Jadyn," she corrected.

"Not when we're alone." He crossed his arms, which just bunched his biceps and distracted her.

"I slept fine. In your bed, if you don't mind."

He flicked a brow with interest. "I mind that I missed that."

She walked around the bed and made a show of examining it. "We could probably do something military. You know, camo comforter, maybe."

"Sure. Wrap the bastard in flag bunting if you want, but don't make me disassemble it."

She lifted the sleeping bag to reveal the hard metal rims that should hold a mattress. "Did you really sleep here?"

"Depends on how you define sleep. I was horizontal with my eyes closed, but…" He rubbed those whiskers furiously before stepping into jeans that were on the floor. "Not a lot of sleep. I'll go hit the head and get dressed at home."

"And Hildie? Will you drive me to her house? Maybe get me a number so I can call ahead because it's early?"

"You don't need a number. She runs an antique shop in town and lives there, literally. And, yes, I'll drive you. But I'm not going souvenir hunting with you. I'll drop you off and go get the lumber for the stairs. Sound good?"

"Sounds great."

He grabbed keys, a wallet, and his phone from the floor and took one more long, scrutinizing look at her. "So how did you sleep in my bed?" he asked.

"Fine, but it was cold. Air comes through that window even when it's closed. You should fix that."

He laughed. "That's my favorite thing about my bed. I usually open the window to sleep and get extra covers in the winter."

"Oh." Something about imagining him in bed, under layers of down, with crisp mountain air… "Well, you're crazy," she said on a laugh.

"No, I just hate rooms. They make me feel hemmed in and cut off."

"Really? I love them. They make me feel comforted and safe."

"Guess that's why you're an interior decorator and I'm a watersports guide." He winked at her and opened the door, stepping outside and leaving her staring at the place where he'd been standing.

"Better be careful, Janie," she whispered to herself, walking around the bed and forcing herself to think of something she could do to save this mess.

Not an hour later, her hopes were buoyed when they walked up to a pink-painted cottage-like storefront called Hildie's House. The covered porch was crowded with knickknacks, random pieces of furniture, a display of Barbie dolls, and a rack of vintage clothing.

"Thrift shop or antique store?" Jane asked.

"Ground zero for town gossip, a place to get or get rid of anything you ever wanted, and guaranteed chocolate chip cookies on the counter for good kids." He grinned at her. "Zane always got one. Every time."

He held the door open for her, and she stepped inside, immediately coddled by the clutter and comfort of the place. It was a mess of inventory, no doubt about it, with chairs stacked on tables and at least six ornate oak breakfronts around the perimeter, each loaded with crystal, tea sets, and china. But in the center, three gaudy chandeliers hung over a fully laid out seating area with a velvet settee, a few mismatched—but precious—antique chairs, and a coffee table in the middle.

This room was utterly wonderful.

"This mess makes me crazy," Adam whispered.

"I love it," she admitted, turning slowly to drink it all in. "Somebody who really understands spatial design put this together."

"Are you kidding? Hildie Fontana?"

"I'm right here!" a woman called from the back room. "One second!"

"Brace yourself," Adam warned. "She's a force of nature. And she talks a *lot*."

"I heard that!" A woman stepped into the showroom with the flair of an aging starlet taking a bow on Broadway. "Adam Tucker, man of my dreams and fantasies."

He laughed. "You say that to all the guys, Hildie."

"Of course I do." She came closer and offered two outstretched arms, each laden with bangles. She wore a multicolored caftan and had snow-white hair that fell in waves to her shoulders. "And it gives me the chance to hug you and shamelessly press your insanely hot body against me for a long and delicious moment." She waggled heavily drawn brows like a professional cougar and flicked her fingers. "Come to Mama, gorgeous."

He laughed, giving her a hug that was far less enthusiastic than the one he received. Then Hildie turned to Jane, clasped her hands, and let out a little whimper of joy. "And who do we have here?"

"Hildie, this is…" He glanced at Jane, hesitating for just a second and making her heart stop when she realized he just might use her real name.

She couldn't take the chance. "Jadyn McAllister," she said, extending her hand. "I love your store."

"Oh, you're too kind!" She clasped her hands to her chest in mock humility. "It's just my little hobby, selling antiques. Mostly I talk to the locals and tourists. Would you like to sit and have tea?"

"No, not me," Adam said quickly. "Jadyn is helping me finish the renovation of the boathouse, and my grandfather said you are the keeper of some memorabilia from the founders. Jane was wondering if she could take a look at it."

"Oh Lord, answered prayers. I need the space and only really want about three things we use for Founders' weekend. I'm the committee chair," she added to Jane.

"When I took over that job about twenty years ago, those men dumped more crap on me than I could stand and wouldn't let me sell it. Then they all got so damn old they can't remember who owns what, and they'd just fight about it if they did. After last month, I swore I would get rid of some of it."

Adam seemed to be backing up with every word. "Then here's your girl. I'm going to buy lumber."

"Take a cookie on your way out." She shooed him off and put a warm hand on Jane's back when the door dinged with his departure. As soon as he was gone, she leaned closer and shot those expressive brows north in question. "Does he kiss as good as he looks?" she asked.

Jane felt blood rush to her face.

"Oh, I figured as much," Hildie said with a clap of satisfaction. "I always had a little crush on his father, Sam. Have you met him?"

"Not yet, but he owns No Man's Land, right?"

She gave a dramatic sigh. "A handsome man who can cook? Such a rare find. He doesn't seem to have any interest in anyone, though. Poor thing. Wife up and left him high and dry. You know, I never really trusted that woman. And I guess I was right, huh? I mean, who leaves their kids and goes off to Hollywood?"

As intriguing as the question—and the subject—was, Jane didn't want to climb into local gossip or Adam's personal business. She knew enough about his mother to confirm she didn't have her priorities in order, and the subject of mothers who abandoned kids was way too tender and too close to home.

She gave a cool smile. "Can I see the memorabilia?"

"Don't you want to know more about Adam?"

"I know enough to get the job done."

"Depends on what job you mean." She hooted a

laugh at her joke and gave Jane a nudge toward the back of the store. "The stuff's out back in a separate garage. Let's go."

When Hildie yanked up an old-school manual garage door to reveal her treasures, Jane literally had to take a step back from the impact of it all. As much as she loved the setup and vibe of the store, the floor-to-ceiling mountain of junk, cartons, and broken furniture looked more daunting than the one she climbed to get to the ridge.

"Oh, this'll take a while."

"Not really. I have a system." She passed by Jane and stepped to the right side, pulling down a plastic bin. "Some of this we use for Founders' Day. Everything in this section is something one of those four men gave me."

"Why don't they keep it?" she asked, gingerly stepping over some shoe boxes to get to Hildie.

"There was talk of a museum once, and of course, I jumped on that. I really wanted to find a place to make an Eagle's Ridge museum, because we need one in this town. There's none other like it in the United States."

"None that I've heard of." But then, Jane was hardly a world traveler.

Hildie beamed. "I've lived here my whole life. My father, husband, and son were all 101st Airborne in the Army. They're all gone now, though."

Jane drew back. "Your son, too?"

Hildie's broad smile faded. "Yeah. He was on an Apache helicopter that went down in Afghanistan."

"I'm so sorry." She reached a hand out, feeling real pain. "I can't imagine how hard it is."

"Hard, yes. But he sacrificed his life for this country and our freedom. My husband and father didn't, but they served, and my Michael—that was my husband—died not long after Mikey Jr. did. Cardiac arrest," she said. "Basically, his heart broke."

"Oh." Jane pressed her hands against her own chest. "That must have been awful."

"Yes, but…" Hildie lifted a shoulder and brought her bright smile back. "I'm a happy woman who loved well and was loved back. Now, over here," she said, pointing to another box. "That's all David's stuff."

Warmed by Hildie's attitude, Jane followed. "Are these the mugs and caps?"

"Oh yes, his precious mugs and caps. And a ton of photographs of all those men, and this box? There's probably a hundred pictures of all the town buildings going up, including this house."

"Wow." Jane dropped to her knees to open one, revealing more stuff. "There's so much."

"That flashlight's from World War II," Hildie said. "And so's that map there."

Jane carefully lifted the paper map, an unexpected shiver rolling over her.

"I know," Hildie said softly. "It feels too important to sell on eBay, though so many of the original owners are gone, or don't remember this stuff is here, or just really wanted someone else to do something with it."

"The museum."

Hildie lowered herself to perch on a straight-backed chair. "I just couldn't do it, not financially and not after my son and husband died. But something needs to be done with this treasure trove of military memories."

"Oh, I agree." And she knew exactly what it could be. "What if I make the boathouse do a little double duty?" Jane suggested. "Sure, it's a dormitory for the kids, but couldn't it also have a historic area, maybe be that museum in the off-season?"

"That's a good idea," Hildie agreed.

"The living area is spacious. We'd just need one wall. I could make a wallpaper out of maps and photos. Maybe add a few built-in shelves for some of this other stuff." She looked around, thinking, getting that zing of excitement when an idea worked. "Maybe even add—"

"The propeller!" Hildie said with a clap.

"What propeller?" she asked.

"From a plane just like Sleepy Time Gal that those guys flew. A friend of one of the founders brought it to town for one of the celebrations, oh, I don't know, fifteen years ago. We used it in the parade a few times, but then it got stored in my attic during a flood, and I bet it's still up there."

"A whole, real propeller?" Visuals flashed in her head. "Can you get it?"

"I can't, but if you send two or three very muscular young men to my house, I bet they could. And I'll watch."

Jane laughed, promised she would, and spent the next few hours happily digging through the town's past and getting an earful of gossip about its present, including some of the names she was starting to recognize.

By the time they were finished, Jane not only had everything she needed to transform the boathouse living area into an Eagle's Ridge mini-museum, she knew that the mechanic shop was going up for sale, Wyatt Chandler's grandmother must have diabetes because she stopped eating doughnuts, the Garrisons were frustrated Ford wouldn't take over the family business, and apparently Diana Woods had a rich and imaginative suitor, but no one, not even Hildie, had any idea who it was.

All in all, a fantastic morning.

Chapter Twelve

Adam leaned back on the last of the beds he'd just assembled and watched Jane work on the maps she'd spread out all over the floor. For hours, she'd been chatting about getting them on the wall and covering them in clear shellac, instead of a mural. At least he no longer had to commission one of those.

He'd given up fighting her ideas. They were too good. And they were nearing a twelve-hour day that had been one of the most productive he'd had in ages. They'd zipped over to some appliance shop in the next town and ordered everything for delivery early next week, did the same with some furniture she liked, and while he installed a cabinet, she lugged all her historical finds into the boathouse and started planning the design.

They broke for dinner at No Man's Land, but that was hours ago, and he was dead on his feet. But she showed no signs of slowing.

"Man, I thought *I* was tenacious," he mused, studying her.

She looked up at the comment. "I thought you wanted progress."

What he wanted was...attention. Hers. But she buzzed like a little bee, humming, talking to herself, moving around, slapping paint chips on different walls, and climbing up and down the loft ladder to get various views.

His view, when not working on beds and cabinets, was mostly of her. Because the harder she worked, the prettier she got.

She'd clipped her hair up, but many loose strands had fallen around her cheeks and neck, giving Adam the urge to sit next to her and brush those silky locks off her cheeks. Maybe unclip it all and run his hands through every sexy inch of her hair.

She wore a simple white T-shirt that he could see right down when she was on her hands and knees, like she was that very second. The angle gave him a glimpse of a lace bra that looked delicate and flimsy and full of soft, round breasts he ached to feel against him.

Her jeans were old, faded, and had little tears in the knees that he wanted to slip his fingers into and tickle her legs.

Yeah. Definitely quittin' time.

"Oh, I haven't seen this one." She gingerly opened a map.

"Don't you think it's time to call it a night?"

"All you've done for days is tell me to start," she said, her attention on the yellowed paper. "So now I'm—oh my God, Adam!" She looked up, eyes wide. "Lieutenant General George S. Patton!"

"What about him?"

"He signed this map." She got up on her knees, extending the map like it was burning her fingers.

"Lemme see."

Still on her knees, she came closer, holding the deeply folded military map toward him. "Is that possible? It's Patton's real signature?"

"Entirely. He was the general who beat the Germans at the Battle of the Bulge. Sounds like the kind of company John Westbrook would keep, even during a war."

"Why on earth would he give up something with a famous general's signature on it?"

He shrugged, taking the map, which was heavily marked and definitely signed, for whatever reason, by Patton himself.

"Should we give it back to him?"

"We can. Or Ryder might want it, if it belongs to a Westbrook. Ask my grandfather first."

She sank down on her knees, much closer to him, right where he wanted her. "You see how bad this town needs a museum?"

Yeah, that idea again. The boathouse as a museum in the off-season. He had to admit it had merit, but it was also the last thing he wanted to think about now.

"Hildie wanted to do it, but after her son died, and then Michael died, she just didn't have the motivation. I should mention this to Harper."

He frowned. "Who's Harper?"

"The new librarian," she said. "Or maybe Ryder, since he's expanding the airport."

Laughing a little, he carefully refolded the map. "Listen to you. Getting to know your way around Eagle's Ridge pretty well."

"Oh, I wish."

He put the map on a box nearby and turned to her, not sure he'd heard right. "You wish you knew your way around here?" He couldn't keep the surprise out of his voice.

And she couldn't keep the faint color out of her cheeks, as if embarrassed at the admission. "I mean, it's a great town. It has deep history. Roots and families and all that military spirit." She attempted a casual shrug and sat down on the floor, crossing her legs. "All this design work has me thinking about the town, I guess."

"Is that what it is?" He searched her face and let their bodies naturally come closer together so that her knees touched his legs. "Or are you getting a little crush on Eagle's Ridge?"

That made her smile. "Maybe a little. This place isn't like anything I've ever experienced before. I've never lived anywhere but…" She caught herself. "Miami."

"Careful, Jane. You might let a new personal fact slip out."

"My bad."

He took her hand and lined her up so they were face-to-face. "No, it's good. You know why?"

"Why?"

"I told you, I only kiss women I know very well. The more I know, the more I can…" He leaned closer and placed the lightest kiss on her forehead. "So, you were born and raised in Miami?"

He heard her sigh. "Yeah."

And he kissed her again. "That wasn't so hard, was it?"

"I've never been west of the Mississippi until this trip."

He drew back. "Really?"

"I've never had money for travel," she said, keeping her face down and not looking at him. "Everything I've had I used to get my education and then start my consulting business. It really only just took off in the last two years, but I had so much work, I couldn't go anywhere."

Letting that sink in, he used his fingertips to tip her chin. "That was a lot of real information," he said with a slight smile. "I'm going to have to kiss you for that."

She smiled back. "Yeah. You better."

He did, slowly, sweetly, barely a real kiss. He wanted to hold back and get more from her. More kisses. More revelations.

When she leaned back, she slipped her lower lip under her teeth as if she were still tasting him. "You're good at that."

"Kissing?"

"Getting me to tell you stuff."

He put his hands on her shoulders and slowly slid them up each side to her neck, threading his fingers into her hair until he reached a clip that he snapped out, and it all came tumbling down. "Your hair kills me."

"In a good way?" She shook her head a little, letting the waves fall.

"In a 'I want to bury myself in it' way."

"Mmm." She leaned into him, turning her head to offer him access to do just that. Pressing his face into the black silk, he inhaled and felt her shudder when he breathed on her neck. "It's my natural hair color."

He lifted his head. "I never doubted that."

She gave him a teasing look. "That was personal information, Adam. It counts."

"Oh, you want to be kissed again."

Smiling, she gave a tiny nod. "Maybe once."

"Maybe twice." He wrapped his arms around her and easily pulled her onto his lap, leaning back into the side of one of the bunk beds as they kissed longer and deeper and with way more intention than they ever had.

His blood instantly heated, leaving his brain and heading south. "See how easy it is to get what you want?" he whispered, tipping her head back to kiss her throat and rub his thumb along her collarbone.

"All I have to do is talk."

"Truth talk," he reminded her. "You can't just make things up to get me to do what you want." He held her gaze while his fingertips slowly trailed down her breastbone, almost not touching her, but he instantly felt her rock slightly in response. "So tell me something, Jane."

She let out the softest breath and dropped her head back a little bit, silent, her bottom sinking a little deeper and heavier on his lap. "That feels good," she said, whispering the words into his ear with a kiss. "I wish it didn't feel quite that good, but it does."

The sexy words tightened him, hardened him, and made her fully aware of what she was doing to him. What they were doing to each other.

But she was still practically a stranger. And that slayed him. "How about your middle name?"

She laughed lightly. "Yours really is Tenacious."

"True." He kissed her some more, turning her a little, inviting her to straddle his hips. Their tongues tangled, and he lost a little control and moved his hand over her breast, rewarded with a moan and a precious budded nipple against his palm.

"Anne," she whispered.

"Jane Anne." He dragged this new information out with the same slow intention he caressed her breast.

"Mmm." She heated up the kiss, taking what she'd earned with her next revelation. "The two plainest names in the world."

"I think Jane Anne is the sexiest..." He thumbed her nipple. "Sweetest..." He settled his other hand on her ass. "Softest name I've ever heard."

She rocked over him, wrapping her arms around his neck for full-body contact. "You're crazy."

"Getting there." He rose and fell as their breathing grew as tight as his jeans. "One more little tidbit of information and the boathouse is going to get christened."

She stilled and lifted her head, meeting his gaze with hooded, heavy, arousal-dark eyes. "Would that be so bad?"

"No, it would be so good. But..." He stroked her breast again, holding her gaze for the fun of watching what one single thumb could do to her. He could do so much more. "You need to know it won't be enough."

She studied him. "You want inside and out, don't you?"

He slipped a finger into sweet, warm cleavage. "Yes, I do."

"Sex isn't enough for you?" Her voice was tight, tentative.

"We can start with sex." He kissed her, delving his finger deeper, growing harder with each silky touch. "But I want to know who you are. What you're made of. Why you are so freaking sexy and vulnerable and..." He moaned, touching a hot, smooth nipple. "Did I mention sexy?"

He felt her stiffen, felt all the sweet melting of her body disappear. "No."

"Jane." He slid his hand up to cup her face. "Jane Anne...whoever you are. What is it that you are so scared of sharing with me?"

She just looked at him, shocking him as her eyes grew moist. "Everything," she echoed. "No one is allowed in. No one."

"Why not?" He searched his brain for a possible reason for her secrecy and came up with only one thing. She wasn't who or what she said at all. That was the only explanation for her wall of silence about so many things.

"Because I draw that line. I'm not sharing my deepest and darkest secrets with you, Adam. My body? Yeah. Please. But that's all."

Disappointment thudded. "I want more," he admitted in a husky voice.

"You think telling you the things I prefer to keep buried is going to make sex better?"

He drew back. "No. I think it's going to make you better."

"I'm fine."

Really. He stroked her cheek, pulling her closer to inhale the sweet, floral scent of her hair and whisper in her ear, "You're not fine, Jane Anne Whoever. You need an emotional lifeline, and I'm just the rescuer to throw it."

She moaned a little, shivered, and pressed her mouth to his shoulder. Then she lifted up her head and looked him right in the eyes. "No, thank you."

Damn it. *Damn it.*

"Then I'll sleep alone." Very slowly, he eased her off his lap, seeing the flash of disappointment in her eyes. Or maybe a little relief. He ached, miserably hard, his whole body humming with the need for release.

His body. Not his brain and not his heart.

A liar, a fake, a woman who could disappear tomorrow and he'd never know where to find her? It didn't matter how much he wanted her.

"I'll walk you back to my place, then sleep in here again tonight."

She closed her eyes. "Okay."

Chapter Thirteen

Fifteen minutes late to meet Ford, Adam hustled past the snack kiosks in the Eagle's Ridge airport terminal. There were enough travelers dragging suitcases away from the small gate area to know Ford's commuter flight, one of only a few commercial flights a day, had landed on time.

Adam had worked with Jane all morning on the boathouse, not in cold quiet but not exactly with her on his lap again, either. By mutual silent agreement, they hadn't discussed how last night had ended. Paint colors, stair placement, and one more argument from her that the shutters had to come down from the windows, but nothing real. Nothing of substance.

The lack of it made his jaw ache from clenching.

He'd lingered on the install of the last of the kitchen cabinets, not anxious to leave her, even though it meant getting some more muscle in the place. But she was deep into her wallpaper map and had started painting color samples on the remaining walls. When he asked if she wanted to come with him, maybe get lunch on the way, she just shook her head and returned to the project in front of her.

Did she feel rejected by him? Angry? Embarrassed?

Or just intractable in her decision to not trust him or let him trust her? Sorry, but he wasn't willing to compromise his principles just for sex with her.

Which might have been the dumbest thing he'd ever done, come to think of it. Sure made for a long and lonely night.

Rounding the corner to a waiting area outside one of two gates, Adam did a double take at the sight of three men talking not far from the gate. It certainly didn't surprise him that Ryder Westbrook would be at the airport he now ran. Adam knew Ford would give his cousin a heads-up that he was coming, even if he wanted to avoid the rest of his family.

But what the holy hell was Wyatt Chandler doing here? The unexpected sight of one of his best friends brought a smile to Adam's face as he headed toward the group. Like Ford, the husky Navy SEAL stood straight and tall, a hoodie covering the muscles he'd built over the years in Special Ops.

The three of them turned as he approached, and Ford was the first to extend a hand for a shake and a fist on the back.

"So much for keeping secrets in Eagle's Ridge," Ford said on an easy laugh. "Got on the plane, and this ugly face was the first one I saw." He shot his thumb at Wyatt.

"Well, there's only two flights in from Spokane a day," Wyatt said. "Had a fifty-fifty chance."

"Not for long," Ryder added.

"Damn. It's good to see you." Adam greeted Wyatt with the same shake and hug, adding an extra punch on the back for his good friend. Neighbors and friends since they were young, they'd always had the bond of being west-side kids, unlike Ford and Ryder, who came from the tonier end of town. "Are my suckass construction skills so legendary you had to get leave to help out?"

Wyatt gave a quick laugh and raked his hair back with a moment's hesitation before answering. "I'm out for good, man."

Out? "You quit the SEALs?"

"You quit the Coast Guard," he reminded him, which took Adam straight back to when they were about eleven and thirteen, hanging out on the river one day and coming across a kayaker in trouble. The save was simple, but the adrenaline rush of a rescue was a high they'd never forgotten.

After that, Adam and Wyatt had talked endlessly about how Wyatt would be a HALO-jumping SEAL and Adam a Coastie AST. Their futures had been set...but now they were changed.

"Well, shit happens," Adam said, wondering if Wyatt's reasons for leaving the military were anything like his. At one look in his friend's whiskey-colored eyes, Adam suspected they were.

"Heard your brother's running a pool for how long until you saw a finger off," Wyatt said, easily changing the subject.

"This one?" He flipped off his friend with a laugh, then nodded to Ryder. "Saw the preconstruction fencing outside, Ryder. When does the expansion start?"

"We break ground today, actually." He gestured toward his work pants, boots, and T-shirt. "I'm pitching in."

"Too bad," Adam said. "I thought maybe you were dressed to help build stairs and..." He glanced at Wyatt, getting an idea that would make one interior designer very happy. "Take down shutters."

"Whatever you need, dude," Wyatt said.

Ryder nodded, taking a step closer. "Seriously, Adam. Bailey told me that your deadline got sawed in half."

"Instead of your arm," Ford added under his breath.

"Yeah, I'm up against it, for sure. And, of course, there's a Zane Tucker bet against me." He shot a grateful look to Wyatt and Ford. "But I'm feeling better about beating his ass now."

"What'd ya bet?" Wyatt asked.

A slow smile pulled at Adam's lips. "Loser has to cover Diana Woods's front porch in roses."

The eruption of laughter could be heard all over the airport, followed by Ryder and Ford fist-bumping at the sheer perfection of the bet.

"Oh, Miss Woody." Wyatt bit his lip and gave a quick air jerk. "How you wrecked our poker game concentration with that fuzzy pink sweater."

Ryder snorted. "The sweater I had to sneak a sticky note on after losing one of Zane's idiotic bets."

"A sticky note with your phone number," Adam reminded him with a hearty laugh.

"Zane's going down," Ford said. "After all the shit he put us through that year?"

"All the more reason you need help," Ryder said. "I can take the weekend off."

Adam blinked in surprise at the offer. He and Ryder had never been close, but they shared a pack of friends. And now they shared a mutual love of Bailey, and the sooner Adam accepted that, the happier his little sister would be.

"That'd be great," he said to Ryder. "Zane'll shit, too."

"He will when Miss Woody finds him up to his ass in rose petals and we got the cameras on," Wyatt said.

"Damn," Ford muttered. "Now I want to stay for that."

"Let's do this," Wyatt said, giving Adam a nudge.

"I'll come over after work tonight," Ryder added.

"Bring beer," Ford told him as he slung a duffel bag over his shoulder. "And remember, not a word to anyone. You didn't see me here."

"Got it." Ryder nodded.

After they said goodbye and headed to Adam's truck, Adam glanced at Wyatt again, still not believing he was here. "Why didn't you tell me you were getting out?" he asked.

Wyatt shrugged as he pulled open the back cab door. "Figured you'd find out soon enough."

"What're you going to do?" Adam asked.

"Not sure yet." Wyatt turned to Ford. "Is Garrison Construction hiring, by any chance?"

"Hell if I know."

Wyatt snorted. "It's only your family, man."

"Family's business, not mine."

"I could use some help finishing the boathouse," Adam said. "Pay sucks, but I'll buy you drinks at Baldie's for a month."

"Whatever," Wyatt said as he yanked a seat belt on.

Adam studied him in the rearview mirror as he fired up the truck. His friend seemed distant, different. He had an almost vacant look Adam remembered all too well after he'd left the Guard.

"You better have gotten good lumber," Ford said as he climbed into the passenger seat. "'Cause I'm building some excellent stairs."

"Actually, you're building stairs that are going to…" He cleared his throat and made his voice distinctly different. "Emulate the mountains."

"What?" Ford choked the question.

"You high or something?" Wyatt asked, meeting Adam's gaze in the rearview mirror.

"Something." He laughed softly. "Brace yourselves, men. There's an interior designer involved, and she has *ideas*."

"Not sure I like the sound of this," Ford said.

But Wyatt was grinning at him. Hell, Wyatt knew him better than anyone. "Don't tell me. She's blond, blue-eyed, and handles an oar like a Viking princess."

Ford cracked up. "You do have a type, Tucker."

"She's not my type," he said. Except when she was.

Jane thought the air was tight and space was small and the electricity fried the air when she was alone with Adam in the boathouse. That was nothing compared to what happened in that space when he walked in with two bruising Navy men who were ready to rock, roll, and finish "this em-effer" in a weekend.

At first, she'd been bowled over. They were both jaw-droppingly hot, built like gym rats who could kill with their bare hands, and hilariously irreverent. After introductions, some ribbing of Adam, and a serious discussion about taking the shutters down that took her to a new level of happy, she got used to having them there. Liked it, too.

She walked them through her plans and rather than roll their eyes or mock her theme, they were remarkably supportive, high-fiving over some Navy memorabilia. Ford actually understood what she wanted to do with the stairs, suggesting risers that were painted like rocks and dirt that led up to a snowy peak at the top.

When Adam told them about the propeller at Hildie's House, it was almost impossible to hold them back from heading over there to get it.

Hours later, the boathouse smelled of paint, wood, and the faint aroma of the burgers Adam had picked up at No Man's Land for lunch.

"You don't care if my dad knows you're in town, Ford, right?" Adam asked while the two of them sawed a long piece of lumber after a lunch break. "'Cause I may have mentioned it when I was over there."

"Five," Ford answered.

"What?"

"We're up to five people who know. You, Ryder, which also means Bailey, Wyatt, and now your dad."

"I know," Jane said, swiping her shellac over the maps.

"But you're not a local," Ford said, making no effort to tell her why he was keeping his presence a secret, and she didn't want to be rude and ask.

"You'd never know it," Wyatt chimed in. "She knows more about this town than I do, and I was raised here."

"Spend a few hours with Hildie Fontana," Jane replied. "You'll know your history."

"I think it's cool," Wyatt said. "I love what you're doing here."

She smiled her thanks and caught Adam's eye, getting a little kick of satisfaction from his smile, too. That had been a little rare today, at least directed at her. He laughed plenty with his friends as they mercilessly shredded each other and themselves. But after last night, he'd been...distant. Guarded. Maybe a little mad at her.

She understood his desire to know more about her, but he didn't understand the can of worms he was trying

153

to open. She was sorry he thought she was holding back personal information, but that wasn't going to change.

Except that sitting on his lap and kissing him just made her want to…let him take down walls. And she'd spent so many years carefully building, tending, and strengthening those walls, she didn't know what would happen when they came down, but it would be—

"Don't you think, J?"

She startled at Adam's question and the latest nickname. But it was easier than remembering what to call her in front of others.

"I'm sorry," she said. "I was concentrating on"—she squinted at the map in front of her—"the Seventh Army attack at the Battle of the Bulge in 1944. How incredibly cool is that?"

"Oh man," Ford groaned. "You need to marry her, stat."

Jane's shoulders tightened as she waited for Adam's groan of disdain. But when one didn't come, she turned to him. He was staring at her, a look of sheer dismay on his face.

Something curled through her, something hot and needy. Something that could make her slip, make her share, make her take down a few bricks. Something that terrified her.

"What?" she asked when he didn't look away.

He shook his head, then seemed to catch himself. "No, I was just thinking that…my grandfather's going to love this. He was there. All the founders were there, and they lost a lot of friends. Fought on Christmas Eve, as the story goes."

"Do you think they would sign some of the pictures for us?"

Adam still had that funny look on his face as he regarded her. "I think they'd like that," he said.

"Not if they all have to come at the same time," Wyatt chimed in from his perch on a fifteen-foot ladder where he was disassembling the shutters. "John Westbrook won't be in the same room as Max Tucker."

"That might be changing," Adam said. "My grandfather wouldn't be alive if not for Ryder Westbrook. Every step we take to make this feud die before they do is a step in the right direction."

Jane beamed at him. "I love that."

"Thanks," he mumbled, then turned back to his task of holding a two-by-four on the sawhorse.

"So you'll tell him?" she asked.

"Sure." He cleared his throat and lifted the two-by-four. "Let's put this one in, Ford."

Jane might have been imagining it, but something had changed Adam. And she wanted to know what. That would probably cost her a little piece of herself.

Which, deep inside, she wanted to give.

Chapter Fourteen

Adam woke at three in the morning because, after a few beers and a day of hard labor, Ford snored like a Rottweiler. Lying on the bunk bed, which now had a mattress thanks to an afternoon delivery, he stared up at the moonlight coming through one of the windows Wyatt had uncovered by taking down the shutters.

Jane had been right about what a difference it made. The light changed everything, bringing the outside in and making the vast area less like a bunker and more like a home.

They had the beds set up in the living area until the stairs were finished, so he couldn't go up to the loft to actually see the view. Shame, since the mountains would be visible and stunning under the full moon that lit the sky.

Restless just thinking about that, he pushed up, the movement causing Ford, ten feet away, to grunt, turn, and rev up his engine again.

Adam sat on the side of the bed for a moment and heaved out a breath. He should be sleeping, but...he ached for something.

Outside, he suspected. Even with the exposed

windows—maybe because of them—he was reminded that he subsisted on gulps of fresh air, the sound of rushing water, and the brisk chill of spring in the Blue Mountains. He needed those things like a man needed food, shelter, and...sex.

That might be what he really ached for tonight.

He'd have to settle for air. Not bothering with shoes or a shirt, he quietly opened the front door and closed his eyes as the first wave of chilly breeze prickled his skin, bracing even through the sweats he wore.

Sucking in the scent of pine and river water, he closed the door behind him and walked toward the boat docks, glancing at the kayaks and rafts bouncing in the moonlight, listening to the soft swish of the calm water lapping against them and, a little farther away, the splash of some current on the other side of the bridge.

He waited for his soul to be soothed, but nothing was soothed. It was stirred, instead, so he walked a little farther, knowing that each step took him closer to the A To Z building, to his apartment upstairs, to the woman...sleeping in his bed.

Nope. No *soothing* with that thought.

Finally, he stopped and turned to look at the window he knew she slept behind. It was dark, of course, and that just made him think about Jane Anne Whoever She Was sound asleep with that silky hair on his pillow and that sexy body between his sheets. He could hear her sigh, imagine her turn, taste the first kiss when he woke her for—

The light came on.

For a second, he didn't move, but stared up at the window knowing that if she looked out, she'd see him in the moonlight. See him stalking her, fantasizing about her, growing hard despite the cold air.

But he didn't move.

Instead, he watched her silhouette rise from the bed and disappear into the darkness, knowing he had the perfect opportunity to get back into the boathouse and not get caught out here. He shouldn't be obsessing about a woman who shared nothing but crumbs about her life. But he sensed her vulnerability and wanted to touch that as much as he wanted to touch every sweet inch of her body. Wanted to know her, help her, rescue her from whatever put that hint of pain in her dark eyes.

But she wouldn't open up.

Of course, neither had he. He blinked into the night as the realization hit. He'd never told anyone the details about the kid he hadn't been able to save. Never confided in a friend or father or sibling what it did to him. Never opened up and let himself be vulnerable.

Was that what it would take?

Her shadow moved again as she climbed back on the bed that was squeezed so tight into an alcove that a person couldn't walk on either side. He could barely stuff the sheets down the sides after he washed them. Which he might not do the first night he slept there again. He might just inhale the essence of her and—

The glass pane moved. A screech that he recognized as the lever that cranked the window. He knew the sound so well from the dozens of nights he'd wake and crave more air. As if he were in that bed next to her, he sucked in deeply, filling his lungs, but not his need.

"How long you going to stand out there, Tucker?" Her voice floated across the expanse, amplified by water and crystal-clear air.

"Until you invite me up, No Name."

In the moonlight, he could see her hand reach out the window and her fingers move, beckoning him.

Swallowing, he hesitated just long enough to know he really had no choice. If he wanted her to open her heart, soul, and body, he'd have to do the same.

His chest grew tighter with each step. He used the keypad entry on the back door of A To Z, then relocked it before making his way to the stairs that led to his apartment. He knew his way, even in the dark. When he turned the doorknob, he realized she must have unlocked the door for him.

Inside, she'd turned the light off again. He took a few steps into the living room, then rounded the kitchen to see the moonlight streaming in over his bed and…his girl.

"You always walk around half dressed in the middle of the night?" she asked.

"It's not that unusual," he admitted, slowly approaching the bed. "I told you I hate rooms."

"Then why'd you come into one?"

"Because you're in it." He reached the bed, his knees against the mattress, his throat tight with anticipation and desire and maybe a little confusion. "I want to tell you something, Jane."

"'Kay."

"I want to tell you something I've never told anyone."

He heard her swallow. "Is this another one of those exchange of information deals you like so much?"

"Yeah."

"Without the kissing." She sounded just a little disappointed.

"Maybe with the kissing."

She laughed softly and patted the quilt that Brenda had made him before he went into the Coast Guard. "Come on. There's room for two."

"I've never had two on this bed," he admitted as he put his weight on the mattress and the bed squeaked a little.

"Really? Why does that surprise me?"

"Because you think I'm some kind of player, I guess." He crawled a little closer, already dizzy from the first scent of something floral and feminine.

"Not really, but I can't imagine you spend a lot of nights alone."

"All of them. At least the ones I spend here." He'd spent them other places after the occasional mediocre date. But he hadn't had a relationship long enough in Eagle's Ridge to bring someone home for the night.

Now, he *still* didn't have a relationship. A fact he sincerely wanted to change.

He finally reached the pillow and put his hand on the glass where most beds would have a headboard. "You closed the window."

"I was freezing. And you..." Her searing palm pressed against his air-cooled bare chest. "Are like ice."

"Not everywhere." He situated himself next to her, but stayed on top of the quilt. If he so much as lined his body up with hers, she'd know exactly how cold he wasn't. While that may have been why he got this invitation, it wasn't the first order of business.

She turned a little, facing him, her eyes glinting with moonlight and arousal. "What do you want to tell me?"

"About the worst day of my life."

She stared at him as that sank in. "Is this because you want quid pro quo information about me that I'm withholding? Or is it because you think I'll sleep with you? Or do you think it'll make you feel better to get this off your chest and I'm a stranger you'll never see again? I want to know your motivation."

For a long time, he didn't answer, because he wanted nothing but the truth to pass his lips. Of course, the answer was *all of the above*, but something was missing from her list. "I feel something for you," he finally whispered. "An attraction? Yes. From the minute I saw you, there was that."

She frowned. "You mocked my makeup and clothes."

"Only because, deep inside, I wanted to mess up your lipstick and take off your pretty white sweater." He placed his hand on her cheek, stroking the silky skin, outlining her jaw, then sliding up to let his fingertip slowly slide over her eyelid. "It just took me a few days."

Her lips curled in a sweet smile that had him wondering just what she had on under these blankets. That didn't help him concentrate on his tale of woe.

"Anyway," he continued. "It's this feeling I have that makes me want to share. More than attraction, maybe you'd call it…connection."

"I understand."

"Do you?" He couldn't help sounding hopeful. "You feel it, too?"

"I feel…" She waited a long time, thinking, searching his face. "Like I went too close to that ridge and I'm leaning over and a good strong wind could push me right off. And then I'd fall."

"And then I'd catch you."

She smiled. "You really *do* want sex."

"That can't surprise you, Jane Anne With No Last Name."

"You don't need a last name to sleep with me, do you?"

"Yes."

She closed her eyes. "Don't make me invent another one."

She would do that? He slipped his hand around the back of her neck, inching her a little closer. "I'm not going to make you do anything. Except listen."

On a sigh, she nestled close to him, letting the quilt be their only barrier. "I am listening."

"On one of my last, well, my very last mission, I lost someone." He'd said the words before, but they still never felt right. Never comprehensible.

"I'm sorry," she said, touching his face, too. "I can only imagine what that does to you."

"No, you can't. You can't imagine the feeling of a body being ripped out of your hands, taken away by a rogue wave, whisked into a storm, and dead at seventeen, all because you didn't move fast enough."

"Adam." She stroked his cheek. "I would bet anything you moved heaven and earth to save that kid. You can't stop the ocean."

"No, but I'm supposed to be able to get someone out of it," he said through clenched teeth. "I could only take one kid at a time, but I knew if I was fast enough, good enough, I could get the other one."

She sat up a little, her hand moving to his shoulder as if she knew he needed to have this story coaxed out. "Where were you? When was this?"

He closed his eyes and fell deeper into her touch. "I was stationed in Kodiak, Alaska," he said. "Best gig of my life. I loved the place, which reminded me of home. The work was hard, the rescues were hairy, my crew was awesome." He stopped for a minute, remembering how settled he'd been. Grounded. Doing what he was meant to do. Surrounded by mountains, water, and purpose. "That job's a coup for any AST because conditions are rough and every mission is a brush with death. You swim in forty-degree water, get some bodies in the basket, and it's a high like no other." Until…it wasn't.

She sank down again, getting closer. "I cannot imagine doing that for a living."

"I can't imagine not doing it." Except…he wasn't. "Anyway, we were out doing training when we got a call that a fishing boat about fifty miles away started taking on water. Stopped training, headed there, and on the way, we found out that the boat had been stolen by some kids."

"Really."

"I know, it sounds stupid, but these kids are so bored. They work in the cannery and have nothing to look forward to. They drink, constantly. Smoke weed, get in trouble."

"What happened?"

"They were capsized by the time we got there. Conditions were bad. Waves were twenty-five to thirty feet, and the wind gusts were at least fifty knots. Bad enough that the CO had to waive the standard and go in anyway, because they were kids and they had no other chance." He closed his eyes, still feeling win buffet him as he hung from the winch cable, fighting with everything to get to the three kids flailing in the turbulent waters. If only there hadn't been *three*.

After a minute, he continued. "It was too windy for a basket to take two, or a litter for one body. I had to carry them on the wire myself, one at a time. I brought one up, no problem. They got the helo right over the other two. I went down, but they were holding on to each other, which was dragging them both under. They started fighting to be next, kicking at each other, taking water, pulling at my gear."

"Panicked?"

"Completely. I just sensed it, you know. I felt it in my bones."

"What?"

"The wave. A big one. Rogue. You do this long enough and you know the rhythm of the sea, and I knew that whoever I took, the other one was probably going to die. I knew it." He squeezed his eyes shut, seeing the desperation in Dalton Butcher's eyes. The plea for life. The fear of death.

"Training kicked in," he said. "I took the one closest and gave the other kid a life preserver. I locked up the first one and hooked us up for the ride. I went straight back down, but just as I hit the water, the wave rolled over and, of course, he lost the life preserver."

"Oh no."

"I was wired with slack so I dove under and got him. I had him. I *had* him, Jane. I could feel his body, his wet clothes, he was alive, and…" He shook his head. "And then I lost him. I tried and tried, but…it just wasn't enough."

"Oh, Adam."

"We found his body about a hundred feet away."

She tightened her grip on him. "But surely you go into this knowing you can't save everyone."

Did he? "I had him, Jane." He heard his voice crack and didn't care. "I had him and lost him."

"In a rogue wave? Aren't those massive? Anyone could be powerless against that."

"But I had him and lost him." It was *his* mistake. "That shouldn't happen."

"But it did. And it's awful for you."

"For *me*? How about his mother?" He could still see the anguish in Nadine Butcher's eyes as she wept over a son who had been lost even before that wave took him away. "She'd tried so hard with that kid. But he was messed up, stuck, miserable. And now he's dead."

Jane braced on her elbow to look down at him. "That's why the boathouse is so important to you. Why you want to make a place for kids like that and give them what you love. The outdoors and freedom and that bone-deep appreciation for the power of nature will give them something to focus on that's not self-destructive."

"Yeah." Wasn't that obvious? "And now they'll have that place." He managed a smile. "And not just any place. A place with a *voice*, as you say."

She ignored the comment, too intent on him. "You need to let go of that guilt, Adam Tucker. You put yourself through AST training four times in order to have the chance to save that boy. A bigger power took him away."

He knew that, deep inside. But still.

"Like you said, that's what you're trained to do. You shouldn't second-guess the choice you made."

He puffed out a breath. "The kid I saved? Joshua Freeman."

"Did he thank you?"

"He shot himself in the head three weeks later."

"Ooof." She grunted. "That's horrible."

"That's what got me. That's when I quit. I was planning to extend my contract to stay in Kodiak, but my time was about up, and I just requested a discharge." Monumentally stupid at halfway to retirement pay, but he'd done it anyway.

"I understand that," she said, the sympathy in her voice as soothing as her touch. "That doesn't make you a quitter, Adam. You're still Tenacious Tuck."

He snorted. "Haven't rescued a person since." He barely whispered the rest of the confession. "Not sure I can."

"What do you mean? You haven't pulled anyone out of that river in two years?"

"I've helped a few dumb tourists who popped out of a vessel while I was lead guide. Not exactly a rescue. Not pulling a drowning person away from death's door. Not risking my life to save one. It hasn't happened yet, but it will."

"And you'll rise to the occasion." She pulled him closer. "I have no doubt of that."

"I better." But he still had some doubt and dreaded the first real test. "Ryder's starting a search-and-rescue team," he said. "He told Zane and me about it first, and I could tell by the way he was looking at me that he expected me to pounce on it. He'll need trained men, he'll need team leaders, he'll need…"

"You."

The you I used to be. "I just told him it sounded great. That's all."

He stabbed his fingers through his hair as exhaustion pressed, and not just because it was the middle of the night. "I don't know what I was thinking," he murmured.

"Not telling Ryder you'd work on a search-and-rescue team?"

"No, telling you all this. Dredging it up. Sharing it."

"You're looking for comfort." She tunneled her fingers into his hair, her hands warm and tender as they ministered sympathy and tenderness. "A way to cope with pain."

"Mmm. Spoken like a person who knows a lot about pain," he said.

She lightly tugged a strand of hair. "Spoken by a person posing a leading question."

He turned, looking at her. "You still aren't going to tell me anything? Going to withhold that last name?"

"So that heartfelt confession *was* quid pro quo."

"Not completely." He held her closer, rubbing his hands over the shape of her body under the quilt. "But I do have to make a decision."

"About what?" She made the decision, and everything else, harder by kissing his chin lightly.

"I could say good night and hold out for a last name—a real one—and more."

"That'd be a dumb decision."

He agreed. "Or we could talk for a few more hours and hold each other until we both fall asleep."

"Uh-huh." She arched her back just enough to press against him. "Getting better."

He inhaled that sweet scent again, moaning as her hand dragged from his face to his chest, caressing his pecs. Blood thrummed, making every nerve ending sing with the need to get under the covers and take comfort and pleasure in a woman whose name he didn't know.

And with each touch of her fingers and spark of her lips, he cared less and less about that.

"What's behind door number three?" she asked.

He reached one hand to the window crank and turned, opening the pane to let the clean, chilled air over them. "I think you'll have to knock and find out."

"Knock, knock." She tapped her knuckles on his chest. "Let me in, Adam Tucker."

"I just did. Now you have to do the same. Name, please."

She kissed him, and instantly he grew achingly hard as their tongues tangled and her hand moved over him.

Fisting the quilt, she pulled it lower to let him inside the cocoon of cotton and woman and warmth. With his sweats still on, he slid in, his hands finding her slender body and pulling it to him. She had on a thin T-shirt that bunched up and gave him access to her soft, sweet skin.

"Tell me your last name, Jane Anne."

She moaned and arched, offering herself completely. Her body, but not her name. Not her truth. Not her trust. He wanted to withdraw and ask again, but his hands had a mind of their own, and they didn't give a rat's ass what her last name was.

He caressed her breast and ribs and hip, finding nothing in his way but a flimsy piece of lace.

"Touch me," she invited. "Touch me, Adam."

He flicked his finger over the lace and watched her face flush with pleasure. And again, slipping under the thong to stroke her. She instantly responded, whimpering and spreading her legs to let him have more.

But he wanted her. All of her. The part of her she wouldn't give. "Please," he moaned, finding that sweet spot that made her shudder and quake. "Please, Jane."

She bit her lip and opened her eyes, looking right into his, her eyes so damn dark he could see his own reflection.

"It's McAllen," she whispered. "Jane Anne McAllen."

Her fingers dipped inside the sweat pants, grazing him. But the impact of her words was even better.

"Can you make love to me now?" she asked.

"Yes," he whispered. "Let me love you, Jane Anne McAllen."

Chapter Fifteen

J ane wasn't the most experienced lover in the world, since sex generally required emotional exposure. But she certainly had never had to *ask* before.

Oddly, it didn't bother her a bit. Maybe because her entire being was consumed by an explosion of sensual pleasures that rolled over her from top to bottom. Adam's hands were capable, talented, and able to make her melt with every caress. His mouth wasn't content to be on hers, but traveled south, licking and sucking and tasting her. His muscles were like granite, every cut and angle something new to explore, and when she stroked the length of him, they both sighed with delight.

He left her briefly to get a condom. Long enough for her to try and catch her breath and tamp down any doubts about telling him her real name. But the fact was, she didn't want to sleep with him until she trusted him implicitly.

Moonlight played over his face as he straddled her and looked down with nothing but desire in his eyes. His jaw clenched, his neck muscles pulled tight, he sheathed himself with a steely, sexy intent.

"It isn't gonna be enough," he murmured as he got closer and cupped her thighs to wrap them around him.

"It's not?"

He shook his head. "I already want more."

If she hadn't been so close to the edge of losing control, she'd have laughed. "So you've said."

"More of you." He entered her slowly, hissing when their bodies joined and letting out a groan as they started to move. "More."

"How much more is there?" She bit her lip as electrical pulses of pleasure crackled as he filled her up.

"So much more, Jane." He rocked slowly, building a rhythm and heat and exquisite pleasure. "More. More. *More*." He kissed her mouth, held her tight, and finally stopped asking for anything as words evaporated into ragged breaths on the precipice of utter satisfaction.

But she could still hear his pleas in her head. As she gave in to the need, felt everything burn, and cried out his name, she could still hear that he wanted more.

The one thing she could never give him.

She clung to him while his body quaked with release, held him against her as they fought for gulps of that crisp oxygen, and finally sighed when he slipped out of her and eased onto his side. Finally, hearts were still and bodies were sated.

Except...*more*.

They lay next to each other in silence, hovering on the edge of sleep and complete satisfaction.

"It's not about the whole FBI thing, is it?"

Adam's question pulled her from a haze of contentment, making her turn to face him. "What?"

"The things you won't tell me. It's not about this drug guy or the FBI. Or at least it's not only about that. Am I right?"

"So you believe me now." She sat up, automatically reaching for the T-shirt she didn't even remember taking off. Closing her fist on the cotton, she lifted it, and he snagged her wrist.

"What are you doing?"

"Getting dressed."

"Why?"

"Because I'm cold."

He gave her a look. "You're scared. You're vulnerable. And you're still steaming from sex, so don't lie to me."

"I'm not lying." But she dropped the T-shirt and snuggled deeper under the quilted covers. "I'm just not going to give you any 'more' like you asked for."

She felt him tense, then relax, sliding his hands over her. "You will. Gimme an hour and you will."

"That's not the 'more' you were talking about."

"True." He moved his hands up and down her body, making her overly sensitive breasts tingle and leaving a path of heat on her now cool skin. "But I will want more of you. Of this." He circled her nipple. "And this." He pressed his lips over her heart. "And this." He tapped the side of her temple. "Am I missing anything?"

So much. "My life. My history. My personal pain."

For a long time, he said nothing, just grazed a finger over her jaw, her lips, down to her throat. He never took his eyes off hers, and she'd never felt more...*connected*. To anyone.

"You'll tell me eventually," he said with quiet confidence. "Because you trust me now."

He might be right. "Do you trust me?" she asked.

He didn't say a word for a long, long time. Then he sighed, kissed her, and whispered, "Yes."

"Then we've made progress."

"Some." He propped up on an elbow, looking down at her. "You're still going to disappear the minute that phone you won't let out of your sight rings."

She couldn't answer, couldn't deny that.

"Is your life so great there that you'd never leave? I mean, now that you've been west of the Mississippi, can't you see how nice it is?" He added a playful grin. "'Specially because I'm here."

She couldn't leave. Couldn't. Then...Susan McAllen would never find her. She closed her eyes as the thought punched her, shameful and stupid and true.

"Sorry," he said, misreading the reaction. "Too much. Too soon. Too fast. We just met."

"It's not that," she said, wanting to reassure him. "It's...other things."

He searched her face, thinking hard, then he inched back. "For God's sake, if you're married, I'll...I'll..."

"No, I'm not married." She smiled at the reaction, though, at how important that was. "I promise," she added. "I'm not married, never have been, barely had any close relationships with men. Just...casual."

He still scrutinized her, harder, in fact. "So I'm not special."

"You're very special," she assured him. "The most special man I've ever met."

"But you're like this with everyone."

She glanced down at their naked bodies. "No, I'm not like this with everyone."

"Secretive. Protective, I mean."

She swallowed and nodded. "Yes, I'm like that with every man, woman, and child." Before he could ask, she put her hand over his mouth. "Don't, Adam. Don't push. Just keep the window open, hold me for the rest of the night, and make love to me when the sun comes up over those mountains."

He closed his eyes and let his head drop against hers.

"I think I just officially fell in love."

She held him, silent, hearing the words, even spoken playfully, over and over in her head.

I think I just officially fell in love.

Funny, so had she.

❧

"Out of the way. Get out of the damn way."

At the sound of his brother's voice, Adam turned from the stair he was nailing into place and did a double take at the sight of Zane, Ryder, and Wyatt struggling to cart a four-blade propeller into the boathouse.

He didn't know what surprised him more—that they actually got it, or that Zane helped.

They managed to get it into the middle of the living room, and everyone who'd come to help, including Dad, Bailey, and Brenda, gathered around the four blades that had a span of about twelve feet and were connected by a bright yellow knob in the middle.

"It's amazing!" Jane exclaimed, practically clapping with delight. "It'll fill almost the whole wall. Can you mount it?"

The three delivery men looked at each other, then at Adam, as if to ask if he knew she was out of her mind.

"What are you doing here?" Adam asked Zane.

"I finished the morning tour, and these two enlisted my help, which they obviously needed." He gestured toward the behemoth propeller. "You sure as hell don't do things the easy way, Adam."

"But you're helping. To lose your own bet."

Zane grinned and started walking around the place, almost tripping over a two-by-four under his huge foot. "Oh hell, I got FOMO."

"What's FOMO?" Dad asked.

"Fear Of Missing Out," Zane supplied, still drinking it all in. "This is incredible, Adam. I can't believe what you've done in here in a few days."

Adam felt a swell of pride at his brother's compliment. "It's all Jane, really."

He glanced at her, seeing her blanch and noting that, for a second, the whole room seemed unnaturally quiet, as if he'd said…oh *shit*.

"Jane?" Bailey asked.

"It's a nickname," Adam said quickly. "I just call her that for short. It's easier than, you know, Jadyn. Hard to say and…"

He could have sworn she swayed for a second, leaning against her map wall a bit for support. "My real name is Jane," she said simply to the group, who seemed to look from one to the other for an explanation. "Jadyn is the name I use professionally. And this professional could not be happier with this find that will absolutely become the centerpiece for the whole room design. Adam, did you tell Zane the theme is 'straighten up and fly right'? So the propeller is perfectly symbolic."

Her lie had been much smoother than his. Remarkably smooth, actually, and it did the trick to fix his mistake and get everyone's attention to shift from her name.

"A rudder would be more symbolic," Ryder said. "You don't actually steer with a prop."

"Yeah?" Wyatt choked a laugh. "You can carry a rudder on your own. I have my limits for free labor."

"Speaking of free," Zane said, plucking at his T-shirt sleeves as if they chafed his muscles. "A To Z is closed for the day, and I'm ready to work."

"You're going to help?" Adam asked, surprised. Zane

had helped with the floor and some of the drywall, but that had been before the bet.

"Why not?" Zane asked. "You still might not win if you don't finish the stairway to heaven." He pointed to the loft, where Ford was hard at work measuring and installing the missing top three stairs.

"He's gonna win," Ford said. "And since I won't be here to see you shame yourself in front of Miss Woody, Wyatt's promised to record the whole thing. And we'll send it to Noah and Jack. Does that cover everyone?"

"Everyone who was in detention with us," Wyatt said. "I may send it to more."

"Don't forget Augie," Ryder said.

"Augie?" Jane asked, looking up from the propeller. "You've never mentioned an eighth guy in your friend group."

"'Cause he's not in our friend group," Adam said quickly.

"That geek wasn't in anyone's friend group," Ford said. "August Kensington was a nerdy little suck-up who took out Miss Woody's trash and tried not to trip over his tongue when he looked at her."

"Didn't we all?" Wyatt joked.

They all laughed, but Adam put a hand on his brother's shoulder. "I appreciate this, man."

Zane grinned. "If you pull this off, you can pay for the roses. What do you need me to do?"

Adam gave a playful punch to his "little" brother's famously large bicep. "You can use that pile of lumber to build a bookshelf or install the fridge."

"Or finish painting," Jane added, holding up her brush.

"I'll tackle the fridge." Zane smiled at her. "I like your real name, by the way. Jane. Rhymes with awesome."

Adam felt his phone vibrate and checked the caller ID. "Speak of the devil from detention."

"Is it Augie?" Wyatt asked, cracking them up.

"Noah." He glanced at the phone and instantly remembered why Noah would be calling him. "I'll take it outside."

There was enough laughter and yakking going on that nobody questioned that, including Jane. Outside in the parking lot, he tapped the phone.

"Hey, Noah. What's up?"

"Adam, I talked to Kenny, my FBI agent roommate, and he did a little snooping around."

"And?"

"He couldn't find an undercover gig in Miami, but it's possible it's very deep. No agent named Lydia, so it's probably an alias. Has she mentioned the name Sergio Valverde?"

"No. She barely mentions her own name, let alone someone else's from Miami. Who is that?"

"He's a major Bolivian drug trafficker who lives in Miami. Pretty easy to pinpoint since that's a fairly tight description. There are others, but he's the biggest, and there *was* an attempt to arrest him not long ago, but not through any undercover op. They thought they had something on him, but the asset disappeared, and everything fizzled. All they have on him now are some parking tickets in Miami Beach."

So the drug guy fit her story, but there was no undercover operation? That made him doubt her again.

"Did you get her real name yet?"

Adam swallowed. Did he need to break that confidence?

"Let me help you make your decision," Noah said, obviously sensing his hesitation. "The missing asset is definitely a woman, and she has the key to bringing down one of the biggest drug trafficking rings on the East Coast. All Kenny could find out is that the last time anyone saw her, she was at the Miami airport."

"You think Jane's the asset? The informer? The one with the information?"

Noah didn't answer for a minute, then, "Look, if you don't think that, then give me her name and let me make sure she's in the clear. Don't you want to know that?"

Did he think that it was even remotely possible that Jane was an informant? A participant in a drug cartel? Not for a minute.

But what if there was no arrest of this guy? Would she stay in Eagle's Ridge indefinitely? Didn't he want her here by her own choice, not because she was stuck by circumstances?

"Jane McAllen."

"'Kay. Got it," Noah said. "Look, I've been called out. Don't know how long I'll be gone, but I'll be in touch, or I'll have Kenny call you if he comes up with anything interesting. Good?"

"Yeah, that'd be great."

"Will do. Talk to you soon."

"You bet. Be careful, man."

"Always." He hung up, and Adam stood staring at the phone, digesting it all. Was it even possible Jane was—

"Adam?" Jane stepped outside, a frown pulling at her brows. "Are you okay?"

"Yeah, yeah." He gave one more puzzled look to the phone, then stuffed it in his pocket.

She came closer, searching his face. "You sure? You look like you just got bad news."

"I'm sure." Which was a lie. He wasn't sure of anything. Especially where she was concerned. "Except…"

He touched her chin, lifting her face to him, scrutinizing it for any sign of someone who'd be involved in drug trafficking, FBI informing, or anything that wasn't pure and good and simple.

"Except what?"

"It's hell being with you all day after last night and not kissing you."

"You don't want any of your friends and family to see you kiss me?"

"I don't care," he said honestly. "I didn't want you to feel awkward."

"You know what's awkward?" She leaned into him. "How much I don't care what they think of us kissing." She nibbled his chin and got on her toes for more. "Also, the helmets are hanging, and you're going to cry at how good they look."

He was going to cry, all right. If he got in any deeper with the wrong woman.

But she slid her hands around his neck, pressed her body against his, and all he wanted was…her. Her body, her mouth, her heart, and her trust.

He took the only one that was available at the moment and kissed the hell out of her, knowing full well at least half the men inside were up in the loft, looking down, laughing their asses off at how far gone he was.

Chapter Sixteen

The boathouse might just have been Jane Anne McAllen's best design work. By Wednesday, all but the final punch list was done, thanks to teamwork that brought together family and friends who all clearly wanted to help Adam's dream come true.

The camaraderie had made the days fly by and the work seem light. And now, with a few days left before the big tour came in, Jane walked through the space with a sense of pride, connection, and affection.

Afternoon sunshine poured in through the three banks of windows that lined the upper half of thirty-foot-high walls. Ford's masterful "mountain stairs" were complete and perfect, thanks to a photographer friend of Brenda's who affixed images of rocks and twigs on the risers to make each step look like a literal mountain path. The effect was absolutely stunning.

Those imaginative stairs led to the dreamiest "campground" loft, ideas courtesy of Adam. He used tent canvas to make partial canopies over the beds, and Jane had used nylon camo-colored comforters that looked like sleeping bags, covering the iron rails she hated.

Bailey found a great deal on potted trees she wanted

for her restaurant, and Jane had placed them strategically between the bunks, finishing the sense that the campers had climbed the mountain for a night under the stars, which were actually twinkling white lights Wyatt had strung from the rafters.

If the upstairs was a celebration of nature, then the downstairs was an homage to the town, its history and spirit. The largest wall was papered in maps and photos from every war and battle fought by a resident of Eagle's Ridge. In the center, the guys had mounted the massive propeller for a breathtaking three-dimensional design element that pulled everything together.

Photos of the four founders were hung between mugs and topped with that "fifty-mission crush" cap. Hildie had even found an old poster online with a World War II plane and the words *Straighten up and fly right* that she'd helped Jane turn into the top of a glass-covered coffee table.

The "mess hall" was authentic, too, with help from Sam Tucker, who donated a lot of the pots, pans, and kitchen supplies from No Man's Land.

"Are you happy with your handiwork?" Adam came up behind her and wrapped his arms around her waist, pulling her into his strong, warm, and now familiar chest.

"Mmm." She tipped her head back, offering him her neck to nibble, loving the feel of his lips on her skin. "Not *my* handiwork. Teamwork."

He lifted his head just before his lips touched down. "So true. Still, if left to my own devices, there'd be primer paint on the walls, shutters on the windows, the equivalent of basement stairs, and maybe—just maybe—a picture on the wall."

She laughed. "You'd have never hung a picture."

"You're right, so credit where credit is due, Miss

Designer." He turned her around and tipped her face toward his. "All I do is inspire you every night."

"Is that what you call it?" Because Jane would call what they did every night hot, steamy, constant, satisfying sex.

He gave a sly smile. "Yeah. You need a little inspiration right now?"

As always, her stomach did a flip. "I always do, but I want to make a point. This wasn't my handiwork alone. Your team was amazing."

"Hell yeah." He nodded and looked around as if he could still see Wyatt up on an extension ladder or Ford nailing each newly sanded step into place. "Even Zane was invaluable."

"Of course, he's your brother."

"But he doesn't lose bets, Jane. Not often anyway, and certainly not to me." He leaned closer and whispered, "What he doesn't know is I always let him win when we were younger because I felt sorry for the sickly little guy. Then, when he outgrew his health issues and got to be the size of a house, I couldn't beat him at anything."

She laughed, well aware of the closeness of the twins, despite their constant jabbing. "Your friends seem to want to beat him, too."

"Oh yeah. And this time, we have. When Miss Woody catches Zane in the act and he feels like an idiot, it'll be sweet retribution for all the times he made us look like morons in front of her."

Still laughing, she tightened her grip on his shoulders and fell a little deeper into his eyes. He dipped his head down and kissed her. "We're done for the day here. The last inspection is tomorrow, then we'll get the signed CO, and I will officially be open for business."

"So now what do you want to do?"

He angled his head and pulled her just a little closer. "I want to go camping."

She pointed to the loft. "You want to christen the campsite?"

"No, I want to go camping. For real. On the ridge. Overnight. Under real stars, with fresh air, and a crackling fire and a sleeping bag shared with my girl."

Her heart wobbled at the words. "Your…girl."

"Woman?" he asked. "I always screw up the PC stuff."

"No, girl is fine. It's just that I've never been… anyone's girl." Her voice hitched at the admission and the powerfully sad truth of it.

"Never?" He frowned. "I find that hard to believe."

She shrugged. "It's true."

"You've never had a boyfriend?"

"Not one that would call me 'his,'" she said. "You know."

"Actually, I don't." That low-grade sound of frustration she now knew so well darkened his voice. He wanted to know more, to know everything about her, but their relationship had slid hard and fast into a sexual one, and that gave her the best and most pleasurable means of intimacy without real intimacy.

He thumbed her lower lip, studying her face. She was used to that scrutiny now, too. She'd never gone back to the motel to get her makeup and hadn't even thought about making herself look her best. When Adam Tucker gazed at her, she felt nothing short of beautiful for the first time since…well, ever.

"I told you I haven't ever been in a serious enough relationship to be 'claimed,'" she said.

"And how's it make you feel to be claimed?" His

voice was husky, but that didn't hide how much he wanted to know the answer. It was in his eyes, his touch, and the breath she knew he held.

"It makes me feel…" She closed her eyes and dug for the truth. "Like I belong somewhere."

"Jane." He inched her chin up to make her look at him. "Sleep with me on the mountain tonight. You'll figure out where you belong."

"That's what I'm afraid of," she confessed.

"Of what?"

"Of—"

"Holy mother of God, look at that, David! It's the prop!"

They whipped around to find Max and David poking their heads in and gazing around in awe.

"I heard it was great in here," David said, pushing farther into the building. "But I thought they said it was like New Zealand."

Max threw him a disgusted look. "Zane said it was like a *museum*," he yelled in his friend's face. "Wear your damn hearing aid, David." Then, to Adam, he asked, "Can we come in?"

"Of course." He broke away from Jane, but kept hold of her hand, walking her closer to the men. "We were going to have a big unveiling for you founders."

Max snorted. "As if John Westbrook would deign to come to this side of the river."

"Grandpa," Adam said. "Let it go. Bailey and Ryder are together now, and the feud has to come to an official end. You going to grumble all the way down the aisle if they get married?"

His face softened. "Fine, fine." His gaze shifted to the wall, and his whole expression brightened. "Well, I'll be damned."

"Come and see it." Jane slipped her arm through his, then beckoned David to join her. "You two gave me the idea for this. A wall of fame if there ever was one."

They leaned on her only a little for support, both of the ninety-something-year-olds moving as if they were magnetically drawn to the wall.

Max reached up and put a weathered hand on the edge of the propeller. "This thing saved my life a few times. Or one just like it."

"Look at this," David said, pulling them closer. "Signed by Patton himself."

Both men stood a little straighter, at attention, as if the ghost of the legendary general stood before them. Chills danced up Jane's arms, the moment taking her breath away.

"Toughest battle of my life," Max said. "The day Westbrook and I were the only two to come back after one mission."

"See?" Adam said, putting an arm around his grandfather. "It's fate that your lives would be forever intertwined."

"Humph." He followed David, and the two of them got close to another map.

"I was there," David said. "Got those planes flying with spit, Vaseline, and prayers."

"Great." Max chuckled. "If I'd a known that, I wouldn't have flown the damn things."

They laughed together, their balding heads bobbing as they shared the memory.

"Come on," Adam whispered, stepping back and bringing Jane with him to the door. "I have an idea."

"You're going to leave them here alone?"

"They won't be alone for long." With the two men deep in a loud and emotional discussion about a war fought and won generations ago, Adam slipped them both out the door. "I'm calling Bailey," he said, pulling out his phone.

"So she can come over?"

He shook his head and put the phone to his ear. "Hey, Bailey, do me a favor. Actually, do yourself a favor." He waited a beat. "Get that boyfriend of yours to drag his grandfather and Will Coleman over to the boathouse as soon as you can. Do not wait."

Another few seconds and she could hear Bailey's rising argument through the phone. "I know you're busy, but listen to me," Adam said in a voice Jane imagined he used a lot when he took charge of his siblings. "You want a big happy wedding with both sides of the family having a lovefest?" He closed his eyes and listened.

"You will, Bailey, and you know it's just a matter of time till Ryder hits his knee. Get the old men over here and you'll thank me later. I'm going camping." Another pause. "I'm taking her with me." And another pause. Jane had no idea what Bailey said, but Adam just smiled into the phone. "Working on it, Sis."

He hung up, slid the phone in his pocket, and put his arm around Jane. "By land or sea? Camper's choice."

She opened her mouth to say the obvious, then closed it again. "I can't swim, Adam."

He considered that. "Okay, we'll go—"

"But you would save me if you had to."

"Yeah, I would." He put his arm around her and started walking. "But with me as the lead, we won't have to."

"Still, I'd trust that you would."

From the look on his face, nothing she said could have made him happier.

185

Chapter Seventeen

"**A**re you recovered yet?"

Adam poked a stick into the fire pit and watched Jane wrap the blanket tighter around herself against the evening chill. "I didn't hate the rapids part. The first one."

"Tapashaw? Yeah, that's great for beginners."

She laughed and pushed back some hair that had dried during the hike. They hadn't flipped, even though the river was a little wilder than he'd expected since the winds picked up.

"And I totally get why you call that rock formation the Middle Finger. Might have given you one when we tipped over so much my face touched water."

He laughed. "We were fine. And you learned all the important tricks."

"Look for the V in the rapids, keep an oar in the water, lean into the current, and have fun. Did I forget one?"

"Don't panic."

She laughed. "The one I can't follow."

"You did great." When he finished stoking the fire, he picked up the bottle of wine and poured her another plastic glassful and took one for himself. Handing a glass to her, he said, "Not much white water in Miami, I guess."

"No, but people do take rowboats through Fairchild Garden."

"Sounds rough, Fairchild Garden."

She chuckled. "There's no waterfall of death, that's for sure."

"Nakanushee? It's like a kiddie slide, Jane."

She rolled her eyes. "For you, maybe. I saw my whole life flash before my eyes."

"You did?" He put his glass on a smooth rock and pulled her closer, his gaze torn between the millions of stars that had finally made an appearance and the eyes that sparked as though they had stars of their own. "And what did you see?"

"I saw..." She inched back. "That was a trick question."

"That was a direct question," he corrected. "When you see your whole life, what are those seminal moments that stand out like snapshots in time?"

Her only response was a soft, shuddering sigh.

"Jane." He pressed a kiss on her head. "I know every inch of you on the outside. I've kissed you, touched you, and made you lose control."

A soft, throaty whimper was her only answer, so he turned his face to her. "C'mon," he coaxed. "Tell me something I don't know. Tell me one memory. Your earliest memory. The very first thing you remember as a child."

She closed her eyes as if he'd struck her. "No."

"And we're back to that." He planted a kiss on her forehead, her nose, her mouth. "It's not a quid pro quo, like you say, but I'll tell you mine. My earliest memory is my mother crying in the middle of the night when

Zane was having an asthma attack. I woke up and heard all the noise, his wheezing, her voice rising in terror, my dad coming in and calming them both down. Then she just sat on his bed and cried like it all overwhelmed her. I remember thinking she didn't *like* being a mother."

"Then we have the same first memory," she said softly.

He eased back, surprised that she was volunteering anything and even more surprised that she had the same memory. "Your first memory is your mother crying?"

"No, my first memory is what showed me my mother didn't like being a mother. But I was too young to realize that. Two, when it happened, actually."

Something in the way she said the words *when it happened* sent a cold chill down his spine. "When what happened?"

She stared ahead, her eyes on the dark horizon, but her heart, he imagined, focused inward. "When a very nice man broke the window of a hundred-and-ten-degree car I was locked in, got me out, and called an ambulance. My first memory was the scream of the siren and my own shrieks calling for my mommy."

He tried to swallow. "Where was she?"

"Inside a house in Hialeah. Buying drugs."

"Oh." It was more of a huff of air than a legitimate response, because…*oh*. "Wow."

"Yeah, it was the beginning of a pretty…" She tried to cover the catch in her throat with a cough. "Rough life."

"What happened? Did they let her keep you? Did she go to jail? Who took care of you?"

"They tried to let her keep me, because that's how it works, and the law attempts to be fair and give mothers a chance to…to…" She smiled wistfully. "Straighten up and fly right."

"Did she?" He wanted her to say yes more than he wanted to take a breath. He couldn't stand to think of this beautiful woman unloved and uncared for.

"No." She took a deep drink of her wine, nearly finishing it before handing him the glass to set on his flat rock. "She was under county supervision, of course, but there were men and more drugs and one weekend I spent home alone in an apartment when I was four."

"Good God," he whispered.

"He didn't seem so good to me," she murmured. "But there is a system in place to help kids like me."

"Did you go into a foster home? Up for adoption?" He was woefully uneducated on that system, but found himself hoping against hope the story got better.

"You can't put a child up for adoption whose mother won't sign away parental rights."

"Even if she's abusive?"

"She never hit me," she said, oddly defensive of this heartless wretch. "But, yes, abusive. In Florida, anyway, the kids are separated from the parent by the county and put into homes."

"Like orphanages?"

"Not like pretty stone buildings with adorable children singing that the sun will come out tomorrow, if that's what you're thinking." She let out a soft, mirthless laugh. "Hollywood's version of orphanages is so…aspirational. They're just homes. Regular houses on the streets, next to other houses, in modest neighborhoods. You would drive by one and never notice it, except you might think the landscaping looked beat-up or the place could use a coat of paint."

He tried to imagine living in a place like that, but couldn't. Not that the Tucker family had been wealthy or even one hundred percent happy, but his home was clean and safe and the family in it was his.

She was quiet for a while, thinking. He stroked the back of her hair, comforting her, coaxing out more.

"Every time she would sort of get her act together, they'd give me back to her, and then she'd screw up again, and I'd go to another home. Never the same one, of course. The point is that your abusive mother can't find you."

"Who was in these homes?"

"They're usually about five, six, maybe seven kids, same gender, close in age. There are county workers who come and go, but someone is there twenty-four hours a day, and local volunteers from churches or just nice, caring people would bring dinner every night." She pulled her legs up, wrapping the blanket all around her as she curled into a ball and rested her chin on her knees. "I was in and out of, oh, five or six of them by the time I was eleven. That's when she went off the deep end."

Sounded to him like that had happened when Jane was two, but he just listened.

"She started stripping, and all that entailed."

He didn't even want to imagine *what* that entailed.

"I was listening the last time the social worker was over. She thought I was asleep, but I was listening." Her voice was barely a whisper, reed thin, stretched by pain. "They were really having it out over me, and then I heard her say…" She closed her eyes, and he saw the first tear fall.

"Jane." Pulling her into him, he embraced her whole balled-up body. "Shhh. You don't have to tell me."

"But you want to know *everything*." Her voice cracked, and his heart did the same thing.

"Not if it hurts you. Not if the memories are going to shred you."

"All memories shred me, Adam," she told him. "The houses, the volunteers, the changing faces and neighborhoods and schools, everything shreds me. I so desperately wanted to be normal, loved, and whole. But I wasn't good enough."

"Jane." He turned her toward him. "Your mother wasn't good enough. You were just perfect."

"No, not perfect. Not..." She swiped her hand over her teary cheek. "She said I was so ugly she couldn't even use me."

He just stared at her, bile rising in his throat as he realized what that she-devil would have used her own daughter for.

"Yeah," she said, reading his expression. "I wasn't even pretty enough for that."

"Oh God."

"The social worker freaked, too, and she fought for me. She got me taken away from my mother, into a system so I could stay in the homes, moving every couple years when I aged up, sent to strange places around Dade County where my mother could never find me. That's the most important thing about those homes—the parents are the enemy."

His whole being felt sick. Helpless. Absolutely disgusted by humanity.

"How did you cope with that?" he asked, a little in awe that she'd turned out so normal and sane.

"I found I had a skill for making things beautiful. Starting with my face, then my room, then the living area, sometimes the backyard. Eventually, I aged out of the system and went to a community college, worked as a receptionist in an architect's office in Coral Gables, then put myself through school. Then started my business." She slid him a look. "Then I got Sergio Valverde as a client, and here I am."

She sucked in a tiny breath as she realized her slip, but he was the one who had to try not to react.

For one crazy second, he almost told her that he'd shared her secret, that he knew Sergio Valverde was a Bolivian drug lord the FBI was after, but they'd lost their asset. It confirmed her story...unless she was the asset.

He shoved the thought away. If he told her, would she be furious that he'd betrayed her? Either way, he had to tell Noah. But not now. Not tonight, for God's sake. Not while she was tender and broken and leaning on him and...looking like a woman who needed love.

Because that's what Jane Anne McAllen needed more than anything. Not sex, love. A person to be her family. A man to protect her. A professional rescuer who wanted to do nothing more than save her, keep her, and never have her leave a home again.

"Jane," he whispered. "Why don't you leave all that behind? Why don't you get away from Miami and move here? As far away as you can get, close to nature, close to..." He cupped her cheek in his hand. "Close to me."

He felt her swallow and try to breathe. "I can't leave Miami."

"Why not?"

She closed her eyes, more tears flowing now. "In case she wants to find me." She sobbed, shaking her head. "I know it's stupid. I know it's wrong. But deep inside, I feel like she might...want me."

"Why don't you look her up?" he asked.

"I have no idea where she is. She disappeared long ago. She could be dead or...anything."

"Hire someone and find out," he suggested. "You should have closure, or a chance to talk to her."

"That's not what I want," she said. "I want her to want me. But I know she never will."

And, he suspected, that made her think no one ever would. And that's where she'd be wrong.

"Oh, baby." He pulled her into him, fighting to contain the crosscurrent of emotions rolling through him. "You don't need her. You need…"

She looked up at him, biting her lip. "I know what you're going to say. But can't you understand how I can't trust anyone, ever? You, of all people, who knows what it feels like to be betrayed by your mother."

"I got over it."

"Did you?"

The volley hit its mark. "I could," he said softly. "With the right person." He looked into her eyes, at the stars reflected there, and the glimmer of…hope. He'd seen that look on a hundred drowning faces, that flash of *Can you really do this? Can you save me?*

"Do you think that's me?" she asked on a raspy whisper.

"Yes, I do." He kissed her gently, tunneling fingers into her hair, pushing the blanket back so it fell behind her. He kissed her throat and chest, pulling her closer. "You're not that little girl anymore."

She looked up at him, uncertain. "She's still in there."

"Let's love her out of there."

A fragile smile tugged at her lips. "You think you can do that?"

"Watch me." Slowly, gently, he began to undress her, letting the night chill and his loving hands create a cascade of chill bumps on every inch of exposed skin. He warmed her with his touch, his mouth, and whispered promises. As their clothes hit the stone, so did that last wall between them.

He unzipped the sleeping bag and cocooned their naked bodies in the envelope of warmth, kissing, touching, exploring the whole time.

"You know everything now," she whispered as he dropped down to taste one sweet breast and fondle the other. "Everything."

He lifted his head to look at her, every last shred of doubt he had falling away. "Thank you for trusting me."

"Thank you for trusting me." She stroked his hair. "And for being patient."

As heat rolled through him, making him ache for her, he felt anything but patient. But this was different. Making love on this mountain, under his stars, with his girl, was unlike anything he'd ever experienced, so he took it slow.

Every touch mattered, every kiss meant something. He inhaled the smell of her mixed with mountain air, dizzy with the effect. She tasted like his favorite place in the world and whispered in his ear like the wind on a breezy day. There was nothing but the two of them, getting closer to heaven with each desperate breath.

"Jane." He said her name for the sheer pleasure of it as he sheathed himself and looked down at her. "My sweet Jane."

"I told you, I've never been anyone's before."

"You're mine now." He lowered himself on her, using his hands to spread her thighs and lift her hips to him. "Will you be mine, Jane?"

As he slid inside her, she held his gaze, her eyes as dark as the sky above with just a little bit of glitter. And tears. The sight of those twisted him and made him stop midstroke.

"No more crying," he said, touching her face and thumbing away the teardrop. "This is good. This is perfect. This is…" *Love.* "Real."

"I'm falling," she whispered. "I feel myself falling."

"I promise I'll catch you, Jane Anne McAllen. I promise I won't let you fall."

"I'm falling in love."

He smiled slowly and moved into her, and out, finding an easy, sexy, perfect rhythm. "So am I," he admitted as they both got closer to the edge. "So am I."

They held on and fell together until they were spent, satisfied, and asleep under the stars.

Chapter Eighteen

"Up. Now. Hurry." Adam woke Jane with desperation in his voice that had nothing to do with a desire for more sex. Wiping sleep away, she frowned at the rapid, purposeful moves of a man who was awake, dressed, and furiously stuffing things into his backpack.

"What's the matter?" Jane asked, blinking sleep—the best sleep she'd ever had in her life—from her eyes.

"Cold front's coming." He half gestured to the sky, barely looking at her. "Fast, too. Did not see this one on the weather reports yesterday and, trust me, you do not want to be up here in a thunderstorm."

She looked up, seeing nothing but blue and some gray clouds way in the distance. "How long until it starts?"

"We have some time to get down the mountain and into the kayak. I'd like to be well past the Middle Finger in a downpour. Plus, Holly had a sunrise tour scheduled, and she could need backup if they don't beat this storm home."

"Oh." She wanted to stretch, beg for a morning kiss, and will the rain away, but she could sense he was serious and focused. "Okay."

He turned away, toward the clouds—or was that just away from her? She tried to shake off the insecurity, be sensible, and remember all the loving, tender endearments, and promises of the night before.

Silent, she found underwear and a bra and put them on while still under the sleeping bag. Then she reached around for her jeans, grabbing the leg, but a belt loop snagged on a rock. When he didn't help, she yanked as hard as she could and freed them, sliding into the cold denim before getting out of the bag. She spied her sweatshirt and pulled it on, then looked for the all-weather boots he'd borrowed from A To Z before they left.

But she was still cold. Icy, in fact, as she watched him pack up their campsite with silent determination and speed. Because people might need to be rescued and he was still worried how he'd handle that.

She wanted to reassure him that she knew he'd be great, but sensed this was not the time, especially when he glanced out to the horizon again with worry etched on every handsome feature.

"Help me finish and let's go."

"Of course." She followed instructions all the way down the mountain, in the kayak, and throughout the whole row home. She tried to find the landmarks she'd remembered seeing on the way up, but this was a slightly different route.

And a slightly different man.

Was he scared of what transpired last night? Having second thoughts of falling so hard and so fast for a virtual stranger? Or just in crisis-aversion mode? She couldn't tell and didn't want to ask.

Rain was pelting by the time they reached A To Z, cold, fat drops that spit on them like the precursor to something much worse. As he climbed out of the kayak and held it steady for her, she thought she saw a glimmer of warmth in his eyes, but Zane came barreling out of the building, calling to Adam.

"We have trouble." He ran faster, his nearly identical features formed in the same hard lines as Adam's. "Holly was on her way back with plenty of time, but one of the rafters hit the southern rapids too hard. Passenger has a gash in his leg and his wife freaked out and now they're caught in the storm."

Adam didn't hesitate, pulling Jane out of the kayak. "You stay in the boathouse."

"Get gear," Zane shouted. "I'll ready up a zodiac."

Adam started running toward the building, throwing off his backpack as he did. She followed, picking it up, more as a way to help than anything else. But something didn't feel right. Something felt light. In the bag? On her?

Her jeans. She patted her pockets, a sudden panic rising. The phone! The phone from Lydia was gone. She'd put it in a watertight case and stuffed it in her jeans pocket, but it was gone.

It must have fallen out when her belt loop had snagged on that rock.

"Adam!" she called as he ran out, carrying gear. "My phone! My phone is on the ridge!"

"Not now, Jane. Not now!" He whooshed by her, hopping into a rubber raft that Zane had already fired up. With a rooster tail of white spray, they blew out, straight under the bridge toward the rapids, leaving her standing in the rain with his backpack, saying a silent prayer for the people in the raft as these two men were literally flying to help them.

Which, of course, only made her care more for him.

Heaving a sigh, she hoisted the backpack, marveling that he could hike with that much weight, and headed into the boathouse, sick about the phone. At least they'd both put their phones in waterproof cases. As soon as the storm was over, they'd hike back up there and find it.

Unless the rain washed it away.

"Oooh." She groaned with disgust and disappointment, digging in the front pocket of his backpack for the boathouse keys. As she did, she felt a vibration inside the bag. Was that her phone? Had he seen it and picked it up while he was packing?

She ripped open the top zipper and spied a waterproof case, which could be hers or his. The case covered most of the phone, so she couldn't tell as she smashed the green flashing button frantically in case it was Lydia.

"Dude, listen to me. Fast and furious 'cause I'm less than a minute from buggin' out for parts unknown." She blinked at the male voice, low and muffled by the case.

"This isn't—"

"Not a good time for me, either, bro, but I had to call you myself after I talked to Kenny. Listen up. That Jane McAllen is up to her ass in trouble."

She felt her jaw drop. Hard.

"She's double-crossing the whole Sergio Valverde operation for one of her own, and the feds want her. Bad. Can you hang on to her until they can get an agent out there and make an arrest?"

She just stared at the phone, her heart clobbering her ribs. Double-crossing... *What?*" She croaked the word trapped in her strangled throat.

"Sorry if this breaks your heart, Romeo, but your babe is armed and dangerous and has some piece of information that could get her a lot of money. Do not trust her, you hear me? Do not trust her as far as you can throw her."

An icy cold wave of horror rolled through her. She was wanted by the feds? Armed and dangerous? Had valuable information? But all those screaming questions paled in comparison to one single thought: Adam betrayed her. He *never* trusted her.

"Adam? For God's sake, are you there? Did you hear any of that?"

With shaking hands, she managed to unsnap the phone case, able to see the screen now. *Noah Coleman.* She'd heard the name. He was one of Adam's childhood friends. One of his detention buddies. Someone with connections—faulty ones—to the feds.

Panic rising with bile in her throat, she stabbed the phone with an unsteady finger, the world shifting under her feet. Go away. Go away. *Go away.*

Dizzy and stunned, she disconnected the call and fought for balance, control, and clear thinking. It took a few seconds, but she caught her breath.

Okay, Adam had screwed her, royally and in every way. Her phone was gone, and the FBI was on the way here because they believed she was double-crossing Valverde's drug ring. She'd never mentioned Valverde...until last night.

Had Adam rolled out of their sleeping bag and texted the info to his friend?

How could he do that to her?

It didn't matter. Nothing mattered but that she get out of here. She spun in a circle, trying to think, to plan, to run fast and far, when her gaze landed on Adam's truck. She held the keys in her hand. Should she run up to his apartment and get her bag? Her purse? Her fake ID and the little cash she had?

What if someone else was in the office? Bailey or Sam? If anyone saw her, she'd have to lie and lie and *lie* again.

Except, she *hadn't* lied to Adam. She'd shared her heart, her fears, and her secrets. And he stomped all over them.

Why should he be any different from anyone else? Wiping a mix of tears and heavy rain from her face as she ran, she tried to tamp down the thought. No time for emotion. No time for regrets. No time for wishing Jane Anne McAllen was worthy of love.

Darting toward the truck and getting in, she glanced at the cup holder that still held her room key.

Thank you, Lord! The shadow of a plan started to take shape as she drove toward the Hideaway Hotel. The keys to her rental car were in her makeup bag, she was certain of it.

She'd leave Adam's truck there, because the last thing she needed to be accused of was auto theft. She'd go to the closest FBI office, in Portland. Then she'd "turn herself in"—for *nothing*—and clear this up with one phone call to Lydia Swann.

Clinging to that shaky plan, she squinted through the windshield, barely able to see because of the rain. Traffic was light and the truck was heavy, but she resisted the urge to floor it. The last thing she needed was to be pulled over for speeding.

Finally, she spied the brown and white battered sign for the Hideaway Hotel. She weaved through the lot to the side of the building where her room was, letting out a soft grunt of relief at the sight of her little blue rental car.

Pulling the truck in next to it, she took a slow, steadying breath. She could do this. She wasn't guilty of anything except trusting Adam. She could find her way to the nearest FBI office and explain everything.

Climbing out with the room key, she slammed the door, remembering how they'd torn out of there the last time...

The last time she fled from law enforcement.

No wonder he hadn't believed her.

At the door, she tried to get the key in the slot, cursing her shaking fingers...and gasping when the door opened from the inside.

"It's about time you showed up."

She blinked away rain, almost falling backward in shock.

"Give me your phone, Jane."

"I don't have it."

Only then did Jane see the gun, as it was lifted and pointed directly at her.

"Give it to me, or you just breathed your last breath."

Where the hell was his truck?

It was the first thing Adam noticed when they finally brought the boats in. The second thing he noticed was the boathouse door was wide open and rain was sluicing inside. There hadn't been a water rescue, since Holly had had the situation pretty well in hand once they got there. But the injured man needed medical attention, and the ambulance was waiting when they tied up.

"I'll be back," Adam said, hustling toward the boathouse with a new wave of worry rising up. She wouldn't attempt to go up the mountain and get her phone, would she?

Inside, he cursed a small puddle on the hardwood by

the door, but his gaze went to his backpack, left gaping open and his phone on the floor next to it, the waterproof case open. What the hell, Jane? Why would she do that?

He picked up the phone, hoping for a message or clue, but the notifications were blank. Wiping it off, he tapped the screen, relieved that it worked. But he still didn't know where she'd gone.

She either went for that phone, which he doubted, or...

Good God in heaven, that drug trafficker found her and took her and—

"Adam." Zane walked in, frowning. "There are two FBI agents out here looking for someone named Jane Anne McAllen."

Adam tried to breathe. Failed. "I'll talk to them."

Zane blocked him. "What the hell is going on?"

"I don't know," he said honestly. "Jane's in trouble."

"Jane? Jadyn? Who is she?"

He wasn't sure anymore. "Let me talk to the agent. Is one named Lydia Swann, by any chance?"

"Lydia what?" Zane stepped in closer. "It's two men. And they are not messing around. They want her."

"Yeah? That makes three of us."

Zane blew out a dark curse and narrowed his eyes. "Maybe you're thinking with the wrong organ where she's concerned."

"Shut up." Adam stepped by him, but Zane grabbed his arm and stopped him.

"What do you really know about her, Bro? Nothing."

He almost reeled at the thought. The woman he held all night? The one he made love to and swore promises to and already started a campaign to beg her to stay? "You're wrong, Zane. I know her and I trust her."

His brother just looked at him like he was a raving

idiot. "You go tell that to the two nice men who want to arrest her."

Son of a *bitch*.

Without another word, he stepped into the light rain where two men dressed in casual clothes stood talking to each other. One was in his mid-fifties, with salt-and-pepper hair and deadly blue eyes. The other was younger, looking around like he'd find his suspect and pounce instantly.

"Are you Adam Tucker?" the older man said, holding out a badge for Adam to examine. "I'm Special Agent Tim Bratcher with the Portland FBI. This is Assistant Special Agent Gary Holcolm. Thanks so much for the tip you sent in to Supervisory Special Agent Murphy in DC. You did the right thing."

The names and barrage of *special agents* all ran together with only one word that really mattered. The *tip*? "What are you talking about?"

"Jane McAllen."

He stared at the man, speechless.

"We've been trying to track down Jane McAllen since she left Miami. Where is she?"

He fought the urge to look at the empty spot where his truck had been. "I'm not sure."

The agent nodded and looked as if he was considering just how much to share with Adam. "Kenny Murphy and I go way back, and he said you're on the right side," the man said. "Jane McAllen has enough information on a chip to stop half the drug trafficking on the East Coast. We need your help locating her *and* that chip. Do you have any idea how we could do that?"

None. Zero. "I left her here a few hours ago, but she…" He finally glanced in the direction of his missing truck. "Might have left to run an errand."

"Any chance she found out you'd turned her in?" Bratcher asked.

Turned her in?

He could feel Zane looming, silent, a few feet away. "Any chance there's been a mistake?" Zane asked, stepping closer.

A rush of gratitude washed over Adam, but Bratcher ignored the question. "We can get a search warrant."

"That's not necessary," Adam said, digging for a legitimate reason not to trust a woman he was falling in love with. Yes, she'd given him a fake name. Yes, she'd zipped out of the motel when the police were there. Yes, his truck had obviously been taken.

But he still trusted her.

Or wanted to.

"Let's go look in my apartment where she's been staying," Adam suggested, gesturing them toward the building and leading the way. He marched into the offices and up the back stairs, opening the door without a key.

"You don't lock your apartment?" the young upstart agent asked.

"I work downstairs," he said gruffly, looking around to see everything exactly as they'd left it. A sweater of hers on the sofa. A T-shirt with some paint stains drying on the sink. And her handbag hooked onto a kitchen chair.

She went without her purse?

"That hers?" Bratcher asked, zeroing in on the same thing. When Adam nodded, the agent reached for it. "May I?"

Adam shrugged. "Sure."

As he unzipped and reached in, the younger agent gestured to a pair of Jane's underwear on the bed. "So how well do you know her?"

Adam just glared at him.

"No phone in here, but here's her wallet," Bratcher said, setting the bag on the chair to unlatch a navy leather woman's billfold. "Lydia Swann," he read.

"What?"

He held the wallet out and showed him. "This her?"

At first glance, yes. Same hair, same eyes, but… "No."

"She ever mention a Lydia Swann to you?"

"She told me the FBI agent who sent her here was named Lydia."

"So she told you everything," the younger agent said.

"Not everything."

Bratcher eyed him, then held up the bag. "We're taking this. And we're going to search every inch of this apartment for that chip, but I'll get the proper paperwork processed. Can you think of anywhere else she'd hide that?"

Her phone. The one she panicked over when it was out of sight.

Oh man. Was he that dumb? Had he been totally played? He refused to believe it, but…things were not looking good.

"Her phone," he said.

"Well, she probably has that on her," the other agent said.

He opened his mouth to tell them where it was, but Bratcher reached into his pocket, getting out a card holder. "Mr. Tucker, if you change your mind."

"Change my mind?"

"About protecting her."

Ire rocked him. "I'm not."

"I'll have a team come up here and look around in case she hid anything in your belongings," the agent said.

"Feel free. I have nothing to hide," he said pointedly.

But did she? He didn't know what or who to believe anymore. His gut said she was innocent of anything they were accusing her of, but the evidence sure as hell was mounting. Where was his *truck*?

"I'll be outside," Adam said, needing a lungful of clean air and answers.

He stomped down the stairs, leaving them behind, trying to make sense of something that made no sense at all. He stormed past the A To Z offices, opened the back door, and walked right into the wall that was Zane.

"Your truck's in the front."

"Really?" He practically knocked his brother over at that news. "Maybe she left a note."

"She didn't." Zane put his hand on Adam's shoulder. "And one of the two-man kayaks is missing."

Adam froze, his gaze automatically looking toward the ridge. She *did* go up there. She did. And she wasn't alone.

And suddenly, he knew exactly who she was with…and why.

He turned to Zane, met his gaze. "I'm going up the back way. You can come with me, or you can go hang out with the FBI who are after the wrong woman. Your choice."

Zane gave him a push. "Let's go. I'm a better climber than you are."

Under any other circumstances, that would have been funny.

Chapter Nineteen

J ane hated to admit it, but Lydia Swann—or
whatever her name was—could hold her own in the
outdoors. Which totally annihilated Jane's feeble
hopes that she could somehow get away from the
woman while on their trek to find the phone.

Escape had seemed possible—and necessary—when
a menacing black pistol was aimed at her chest and the
no-nonsense FBI agent showed a deadly intent to use it.
In seconds, Jane had realized there was no way she was
an FBI agent...and no way to run from the woman or the
question she wouldn't stop asking: Where was the
phone?

Saying she'd lost it just got that gun raised a little
higher toward Jane's head. Admitting she knew where it
was got Jane pushed back into the truck with an order to
drive. Learning that getting it meant rapids, waterfalls,
danger, and a muddy hike didn't deter Lydia one single
bit.

Jane had sped back to A To Z, managing to drive
despite the heavy silence and heavier revolver still aimed
at her. But, sadly, no Eagle's Ridge police officer pulled
her over. She prayed Adam or someone would be at the
office, but Adam and Zane were still out on their

mission and the office looked deserted. She hoped against hope that the rapids would take Lydia, that the Middle Finger rock formation would spill their kayak, or that a bad ride down the Nakanushee Falls would end this nightmare.

None of that happened, since Lydia was clearly versed in the art of giving orders, handling an oar, and never putting that damn gun down.

Now they were sloshing their way up a mud-covered path, and the skies were as threatening as her hiking partner. A flash of lightning in the distance announced that this band of rain included thunderstorms.

Trust me, you do not want to be up here in a thunderstorm.

The problem was, she *had* trusted him. And he'd shared her secret with someone, and…now Lydia Swann was ready to kill her for a phone?

"What if the phone's gone?" Jane asked as she tried to cling to a branch to keep her boot from sliding and taking her down the side of the mountain.

"Then you will be, too."

Jane slipped and lost hold of the branch, falling into Lydia, who kept her balance. "If it's so important to you, why did you let me cart it across the country?"

"I had to get it out of Miami by someone who wasn't me. You fit into the plan perfectly."

The plan? "You planned this?"

"The day I saw you, I knew you were my ticket."

Jane's steps slowed as she tried to catch her breath and make sense of what the woman said. "To what?"

Lydia gave her a hard nudge forward. "Just move. Fast."

Jane tripped again, using her hands to break the fall, covering her palms in cold, sticky, unforgiving mud.

"Why are you doing this?" she cried as she attempted and failed to get her footing. "What are you trying to accomplish?"

"How much farther?" Lydia demanded, looking past Jane and up the mountain.

Jane followed her gaze, seeing the boulder she knew marked the end of the "safe" trail and the beginning of the last treacherous section of the path before reaching the ridge. "After we climb that," she said, gasping for a breath. "Around…then…we'll be there."

"Good. Good. We're almost done."

"Done with what?" Jane demanded.

Lydia threw her a vile look, then reached down and grabbed the collar of the down vest Jane had put on hours ago, not far from here, at the campsite.

"Get moving or die."

"I'm not much good to you dead," she muttered, pushing herself up in the world's most graceless rise. "But I sure was good to you alive. Why me, for God's sake? I'm an interior designer. Why?"

"Look at you," she said. "Same hair and eye color. Even the same height. The ID switch was easy."

Jane tried to process that as they neared the boulder, remembering how generous the offer had seemed at the time. *Take my ID*, Lydia had said that hectic night at the airport. *We look enough alike. You can't have yours on you anyway.*

And Jane, like a trusting idiot, handed over everything she had that said Jane Anne McAllen on it.

"So you targeted me to switch ID's and sent me off with a phone that you'd kill for?" Her voice rose in wild frustration. "Why would you do that?"

She jabbed Jane with the gun. "Don't even try to yell for help."

210

As if anyone would hear. As if Adam would come after her. The knowledge that he wouldn't, that by now he surely believed the worst about her, believed that…what had that man said on the phone? *She's double-crossing the whole Sergio Valverde operation for one of her own, and the feds want her. Bad.*

"So you're screwing Sergio," Jane said.

"Not technically," she replied dryly. "I draw the line at sex with the scumbag bastard who killed my father."

"But…professionally?" she guessed, earning a look of begrudging respect from her nemesis.

"I'm doing what I have to do to put Sergio Valverde out of business and take everything owed to me."

"And the phone?"

"It has what I need to do that."

They reached the boulder and stopped cold, and even Lydia was a little winded. Or maybe emotional.

Sergio killed her father? Jane filed that away as a possible weapon.

"Climb it." She shoved the pistol into Jane's kidney.

Of course, emotional currency was hardly as effective as that gun. "It's hard," she said. "Especially in muddy boots."

Lydia's dark eyes narrowed to cold, black slits. "It'll be really hard when you're dead."

Jane turned and found the crevice she'd used the first time she'd climbed this particular obstacle. Back when she was falling for Adam. Trusting him. Counting on him. Actually letting herself fall in love with him.

And he sure as hell wasn't going to come and save her, so she damn well better do it herself.

At the fury of that thought, she swung herself up, making it easily in one move, turning quickly to see Lydia, who had stuck the gun in her pants and, for one second, was looking down to find her footing.

Now. Now was her chance. There was only one place Lydia could put her hand. One stone to use as a grip. Taking a deep breath, she stole a glance to her left, where Adam had blocked any chance of her falling. Not a particularly steep fall, but it was mud, and Lydia would go tumbling at least fifty feet. Enough time for Jane to run.

Bracing for support, she stared at Lydia's hand rising, moving as if in slow motion, higher, higher, over her head and away from that pistol, and landing on the stone.

Jane lifted her muddy boot and slammed it down so hard she could have sworn she heard bones crack but for Lydia's howl in pain. Instantly, Lydia lost her balance and Jane jumped right back down and pushed with all her might, knocking the other woman to the side, but not over the edge.

Damn it!

Lydia swung around, using her leg, but Jane got a hold of that and thrust her whole body into a push. Lydia screamed, reached for her pistol, but fell backward. Jane took one last swipe, and down Lydia went, ass first, hands and feet in the air, screaming and sliding down the muddy side of the mountain.

Jane froze for one second in shock, then turned and ran, falling and slipping and swearing as she made her way back down. She heard Lydia's screams echo off the mountain and the cliff, and then a single, heart-stopping gunshot told her the woman hadn't lost her weapon.

Fastest way. Fastest way. By boat, of course, without a life jacket and only one person in the boat.

Jane ran, fell, rolled, scraped her face, but pushed right back up and fought her way to the bottom of the path.

ADAM

She heard the rushing water and knew she was one step closer to safety. She could hide, of course, but Lydia would find her. She had to strand Lydia with no boat. Only a local would know the footpath out of there.

A huge bolt of lightning made her stumble again, followed by thunder and...another gunshot. Did Lydia already have her in her sights?

Jane reached the two-man kayak they'd stolen and dived toward it, scrambling inside and grabbing one of the oars, nearly dropping it as she tried to push off from the rocky shore.

The rain pelted and the skies lit up with another bolt of lightning, but Jane ignored nature's fury and pushed with all the strength she had, finally getting the boat off the shore.

The white, rushing, wild water suddenly seemed a thousand times more dangerous than on the way here, when her focus had been on that gun aimed at her back.

The kayak rocked and swayed and bounced along on the water, icy spray pricking her face and body like little knife tips. A wave crested over the tip of the kayak, making Jane scream as she bounced down so hard her teeth knocked together.

Another flash of lightning, followed by a much-too-close thunderclap, stole what breath she had left, firing her with the strength to use the oar and remember the most basic things Adam had taught her to stay alive.

Aim the boat at the V in the rapid. Keep the paddle in water. Lean into the current. Don't panic.

Too late.

At the pop of a gunshot, she ducked instinctively and stole a glance over her shoulder, catching sight of Lydia on the riverbank, her pistol aimed dead ahead at Jane.

The only thing keeping her alive was the wild waves,

bouncing her so crazily she was a moving target. Peering through the rain, she spied the vertical jut of a distinct rock formation.

The Middle Finger. If she could just get by that, around those rocks without flipping, she'd be out of sight.

Find the V. Paddle in water. Don't panic.

She stabbed the rapids with the oar and thrust her body forward, trying to force the kayak into the V of the two converging rapids, gasping for air as another chilling splash hit her face. Bracing for the next bullet, she stayed as low as she could, her gaze locked on that rock.

If she could just get to it, get past it. She heard a shriek, followed by another gunshot, making her duck again.

A sudden wave rose up and lifted the kayak, balancing it high, then the kayak leaned left and...more left...and then she was completely sideways, suspended in air for one split second. She opened her mouth to scream in horror, but she hit the water so hard it was like crashing onto ice, then instantly there was darkness and the roar of water and a freezing wet force that dragged her and bounced her and refused to let her go.

The water was stronger than she'd ever dreamed. More vicious and powerful than her worst nightmare. It grabbed her and flung her and choked her.

No, that wasn't water. It was an arm, clamped around her neck, pulling her up, dragging her.

Lydia got her!

She fought wildly, kicked, and took in a lungful of water. She couldn't get to the surface. She couldn't breathe. The force pulling her was stronger and more determined and completely in charge. She fought with everything she had, kicking, pulling, refusing to be overpowered.

But water filled her lungs and she was absolutely no match for the strength of her attacker. Blackness closed in, dragging her into oblivion and certain death.

Chapter Twenty

*J*ane! *Come on, damn it. Come on! Quit fighting me!*
Finally, her body went limp under Adam's rescue grip, but the rapids were relentless, pounding them both and taking them farther from shore.

He battled to keep her head above water, fully aware she'd passed out and could easily drown. And die.

She can't die. She can't die. She can't die.

The mantra echoed in his head, louder than the rushing water, stronger than the brutal current. She had to live, so he could tell her that he trusted her, believed her, and fought for her. He'd heard the first scream just as he and Zane reached the top of the ridge and spied the phone wedged among the rocks of the fire pit.

Without hesitating, he'd run in the direction of the sound, hustling down the path and over the boulder to spot a woman who wasn't Jane clawing her way back up and running down the path, gun drawn.

She beat him to the bottom and started shooting before Adam knocked her on her ass. When he looked up, he saw the kayak flip right into the icy water. That's when he left the woman for Zane to deal with and started swimming for his life.

No, for *hers*.

She can't die. She can't *die.*

With each thought, he kicked and clawed, clinging to her lifeless body, bracing for the next rapid to crash over them. He knew the waves and rocks, knew what to expect, knew he could get her back to shore.

He started kicking harder and harder, one hand outstretched in anticipation of a rock. He heard it first, like thunder in his ears. And then he felt it instinctively. Just as he came up for air, he saw it. A massive wall of white water, a roller wave coming right at them.

He'd seen them here before, not uncommon with the ledge near the Middle Finger that reversed the current and gave a wild ride. Experienced rafters prayed for the adventure of this kind of wave. Someone swimming with a lifeless victim prayed to survive it.

The noise deafened, and he turned to hold Jane with both arms, bracing for the impact as the wave knocked over both of them, slamming them, crushing them, and trying to pull Jane away from him with tons of power.

Her body dragged, almost out of his arms, almost lost. But he gritted his teeth and fought for her.

She can't die!

And then the wave was past, replaced by quieter ruffles, easy froth, and the knowledge that he hadn't lost his grip. He swam them to the riverbank and got her on her back, ignoring the rain and lightning, but the storm was already moving on.

"Come on, Jane. Breathe!" He turned her head to drain her mouth and nose of water, his heart breaking at the sight of gashes and scrapes on her cheeks.

Clearing her airway, he put his mouth over hers, held her nose, and breathed out a lungful of air into her. He felt for a pulse, waited for the miracle.

He couldn't lose her. He couldn't. He had to tell her

he believed her. He trusted her. He wanted her in his life forever.

Once again, he inhaled and transferred every molecule of air to her, holding her as he felt her slip away.

"No, Jane. Don't. Don't leave me. Don't—"

She moaned. Rolled her head from side to side. And suddenly, she expelled the water from her lungs.

"Yes!" He lifted her gently. "There you go. That's my girl."

She groaned in agony, still limp in his arms. "Adam…"

"I'm here, Jane. I'm here."

"Your…girl." Her eyes barely fluttered open, closed again, and her head fell back in complete relief. "Adam."

He wrapped her shivering, waterlogged body in his arms and squeezed so tight he could feel her shuddering bones. "You made it. You did it. You beat her."

She managed to lift her head, her mouth still open as she gasped for air, her eyes slits under thick, wet lashes. "You be…believe me."

"Yes," he said simply. "I believe you."

Quivering, she leaned into him, her teeth chattering like a jackhammer. "Where is she? That monster? She wanted to ki-ki-kill me."

At the farthest end of the shore, well out of hearing with the rushing water, Zane held the woman in one mighty arm, a phone to his ear as he no doubt called for backup. "Zane has her."

She opened one eye a little more. "How?"

"I told you there's a back way by rock-climbing. We beat you there, found the phone, and heard you scream."

"How did you know about her?"

"The FBI came to arrest you."

She closed her eyes. "You told Noah."

"Jane, I'm sorry. I thought I was protecting you, clearing you. She used your ID, didn't she?"

She nodded, looking away, hurt in her eyes.

"I'm really sorry," he said again. "I wanted to help you."

She finally looked back at him, and with strength he'd doubted she even had, she lifted her hand and touched his cheek. "I wanted to trust you."

He scooped her higher into his chest. "You can. I'm here for you. I'll defend you no matter what happens."

"There's nothing to defend, Adam."

"I know." He kissed her head again. "I know." In the distance, he heard a familiar thud of blades in the air. "Help is coming. Ryder in the rescue helicopter. And the FBI."

Her eyes flashed.

"I'll kill them with my bare hands before they accuse you of anything."

She managed a smile at his over-the-top promise. "Thanks."

He dropped his forehead against hers. "You know this could be it for us."

"The end?"

He lifted up and looked at her. "The beginning. It's all up to you."

"Okay." She closed her eyes and gave in to another shiver, holding him with weakened arms as the chopper came into sight. "And, Adam?"

"Yeah?"

"Thanks for the rescue."

But deep in his heart, he knew he should be thanking her for the same thing.

"Coleman Medical Center?" Jane read the name on the nurse's scrubs as the woman wheeled her cart of medical supplies out of the emergency treatment room where she'd been tending to Jane. "As in Noah Coleman?"

Next to her bed, Adam stepped forward. "And Will Coleman, one of the founders of Eagle's Ridge."

She angled her head to see him. Someone had brought him dry clothes, and he must have changed while she was in triage. That was the only time since he'd saved her that they'd been apart. He wouldn't leave her side.

"Noah thinks I'm some kind of criminal," she said.

"I'll set him straight next time I talk to him," Adam said, leaning over the bed to kiss her on the forehead. "I'll set anyone straight who even—"

A tap on the door made him stand, and it opened slowly as a man walked in, steely blue eyes trained on Jane. "Ms. McAllen? Special Agent Tim Bratcher. Can I talk to you?"

She recognized the name of the FBI agent Adam had told her about in the helicopter, but the details were fuzzy back then.

"Yes, come in," she said, sitting higher and adjusting the hospital gown they'd changed her into.

The man nodded to Adam in silent recognition. "Thanks to both of you for a job well done."

Jane felt a frown form, then glanced up at Adam. "What did we do?"

"You brought in a woman we've wanted for a long time, and that phone you kept with you all this time had information that will lead us to some of the top drug trafficking rings in the country."

"Lydia Swann?" she asked.

"That's one of her names," he told her. "One of about twenty. Her real name is Alana Cuevas, the daughter of a Colombian drug lord killed by Valverde. She's been planning to bring him down since she was a teenager. She worked her way into his circle, stole valuable contact information, then told Valverde you had it."

"And I did," she said. "At least I assume that's why she wanted the phone."

"Exactly. The chip was inside."

"Why would she give it to me?" Jane asked.

"To get the information out and safe and set you up. She put a target on your back with Valverde who would know that he'd been screwed by someone. Your similar looks worked perfectly for her to arrange it all and make you look like the bad guy."

Jane tried to take all that in, barely able to. "But she had so much information on me," she said softly, remembering all that Lydia Swann had known when she sent Jane off to Washington. About her childhood and the homes. "How?"

"She's a computer whiz and has a specialty for data mining. No doubt she wanted to know enough about you to be sure you didn't have a family who'd come after you. She needed someone she knew would follow her orders."

Sighing, Jane closed her eyes. "I was stupid."

"You were smart," Adam countered. "You were trying to protect yourself."

The agent nodded as if he agreed. "She'd have let you take the fall with Valverde in a heartbeat," he said. "If her plan hadn't gone awry, I'm certain she'd have let him know you were the mole and told him exactly where to find you."

She shuddered at the thought. "How did it go awry?" she asked.

"The night before she left, we moved in on his operation. She wasn't there, but got wind of it and took off after you. When you didn't have the phone, she panicked and obviously tried to kill you."

Adam's grip tightened. "We weren't about to let that happen."

"And you are free to go back to Miami, ma'am," Bratcher said. "Valverde is in custody, too. Would you like us to arrange a flight for you?"

"No," she whispered, threading her fingers through Adam's. "I think I'm going to stay here for a while."

Bratcher nodded and gave what she suspected was a rare smile. "If there's anything I can do for you, then," he said, "just ask."

"No, I—"

"Yes, there is," Adam said, giving her hand the lightest squeeze.

"Name it."

"We could use some help finding someone named Susan McAllen."

A wash of gratitude rolled over Jane as Adam uttered her mother's name. She looked up at him and saw that tenacity on his strong features she'd come to adore. He wanted to help her, to rescue her, to offer her closure from her past, and that touched her heart.

"Your mother?" the FBI agent asked Jane. At her surprised look, he tipped his head. "We did some research on Susan McAllen when we thought you were a suspect."

She stared at him for a moment, knowing that he probably knew exactly where her mother was. All she had to do was ask and then…

She swallowed and gave her head a quick, negative shake. "I don't need that information," she said, looking up at Adam, a rush of love warming her. "I have everything I need now."

And for the first time in as long as she could remember, she meant it.

The agent shook their hands and left, closing the door with a firm click.

Adam took a step so he could look into her eyes. "Are you sure you don't want to go back?"

"I'm sure." She reached up and touched his cheek. "I'm right where I want to be."

Epilogue

They waited until it was after midnight and moved like ninjas down the residential street on the outskirts of Eagle's Ridge. Well, three of them did.

Zane clomped his big ass down the middle of the street, his arms laden with the bouquets of roses Adam had arranged to have delivered to A To Z earlier that day. Paying for the bet was the least he could do, since he hadn't won it fair and square. And wouldn't have won at all without Zane's help.

Plus, the big lug had taken down a criminal to help save Jane, so at least Adam should cough up a few hundred for the stunt. He did it anonymously, of course, so Diana couldn't ever find out which of them paid, but the cost was worth five times that to see his gambling brother lose a bet.

"They gotta be everywhere, Zane," Adam called in a hushed whisper, holding back with Ryder and Wyatt. "Piles of those suckers all over the porch."

"I know, I know. I came up with the idea, remember?"

"And we are not bailing you out when you get caught," Wyatt added. "We're just getting some evidence and then we're out."

Jane was waiting at the cross street in Adam's truck

with Bailey. The minute the guys had recorded evidence—and made a little noise to wake up Miss Woody—they would all hop in the truck and take off, leaving Zane to fend for himself.

"He so deserves this," Ryder said.

"I just wish Noah, Jack, and Ford were here to see," Wyatt said.

"I'll have the proof on my phone," Adam assured them.

They came to her house, a cute little Craftsman-style bungalow with a front porch and swing, and not a single light on.

"I don't want to scare her." Adam slowed his step, thinking of how Jane would feel hearing a strange noise in the middle of the night.

"I'll just throw a little pebble up at her bedroom window," Wyatt said.

"You know which room's her bedroom?" Ryder asked.

Wyatt gave a low chuckle. "I did a few drive-bys in high school."

"Loser," Zane called over his shoulder, obviously hearing every word.

"Like you didn't," Wyatt shot back.

"*I* sure as hell didn't," Adam said. "Did you, Ryder?"

"Hell no. I had plenty of dates in high school. Didn't need to stalk Miss Woody."

Adam rolled his eyes. "Of course, BMOC wouldn't have problems getting a date."

He shot Adam a look. "I'm done dating, unless it's date night with my…" He just smiled. "*Way* more than significant other."

Adam couldn't help smiling back. "Bailey's happy. I'm glad for you guys."

"And what about you?" Ryder asked.

"He's finished," Zane called over his shoulder. "DOA. Jane-not-Jadyn is the one."

Ryder eyed him. "Happens fast, right?"

"It can," Adam agreed.

"Good," Ryder said. "You got your ass nice and settled down and the boathouse is finished."

Adam nodded. "All except for one thing. That offer to work reserve on your search-and-rescue team still open?"

"Hell yeah." Ryder held up his knuckles for a congratulatory tap. "I wondered why the hell you didn't scoop that up. I'm going to need you, man."

"You got me." Adam just closed his eyes for a minute, trying to let that sink in and—

"All right. Shut up. All of you." Zane practically stomped his foot delivering the order. Wyatt, Ryder, and Adam held back, watching the big man march up a few stairs as the three of them hid like hoodlums behind some bushes.

"Everywhere!" Adam called, his phone out and recording video.

With his free hand, Zane shot him the bird, tossing roses with the other.

"The window, Wyatt," Ryder reminded him.

"I'm on it." Wyatt scooped up some gravel and backed up, tossing a few pebbles at an upstairs window.

The bedroom light came on instantly, and the he-man on the porch was making enough noise that it was only a few seconds until the front porch—and Zane—was bathed in light.

Adam, Wyatt, and Ryder silently guffawed and exchanged a few high fives.

"Record the shit out of this," Wyatt said.

"I got it, I got it," Adam assured him, holding the phone high over the shrubs just as the front door opened. Ryder almost doubled over in laughter he fought to keep quiet.

"What are you—"

"Oh, Miss Woody, I mean, Woods, I mean, Diana."

Wyatt nearly fell on the ground he was laughing so hard.

"Zane Tucker?" The familiar voice that brought back hours in detention hall floated through the night air. "What on earth are you... Are those roses?"

"Um, yes, ma'am, they are."

"I'm gonna die," Ryder whispered, fighting hysteria.

"And should I call the police and perhaps have you talk to Lieutenant Stonecipher about why you are trespassing and defacing my property in the middle of the night?"

"Ooh, she's so hot when she's pissed." Wyatt punched Adam and made the phone wobble, but it was forgivable, because moments like this happened once in a lifetime.

"No, ma'am, you should not call him." Zane's voice reached him loud and clear. "This is not trespassing or defacing."

"Like hell it's not," Ryder mumbled between laughs.

"What would you call it? A new service in town? Midnight flower delivery?" She always did have a wicked sense of humor, which only made the woman more attractive.

"I'd call it..." He cleared his throat. "A favor from a secret admirer."

"Not so secret," Wyatt whispered.

"Is that so?" Miss Woody asked. "Well, considering the circumstances, I'd like a little proof of that, if you

227

don't mind. Maybe take the *secret* out of secret admirer?"

Wyatt and Adam looked at each other. "He's so screwed," they whispered in unison.

"Well, I can show you the receipt. You can see that these weren't purchased by me, but by an anonymous, uh, suitor. Here, let me show you."

Zane had the receipt? Son of a bitch.

"'Paid in cash,'" she read. "By 'a secret admirer.'"

"Um, yes," Zane said. "I'm doing this as a favor for a friend."

"Who might that be?" Miss Woody demanded, a little of the edge gone in her voice.

"I can't say, ma'am. Because, well, if I told you, he'd have me killed."

She choked a soft laugh.

"But he sent this with his love, and I had to help the guy out, you know. He's shy and isn't sure how you'd feel about his interest."

"Oh, Zane." Her soft sigh drifted their way. "That's so sweet."

"But he is smitten, ma'am. I can tell you that."

"Well, that's very…" She laughed a little self-consciously. "You sure you won't tell me who it is? This is starting to get a little…curious."

"I can't break the code of honor, Miss Woods. I'm sure you understand."

"You've always been such a good guy, Zane Tucker."

Adam, Wyatt, and Ryder looked at each other in shock and disgust.

"I see that hasn't changed as you've grown older. Thank you. This gesture has made my night."

Zane backed away, giving a half nod-bow thing like

he was some kind of hero. "My pleasure, ma'am. Good night, now."

"Good night." She bent over and took one of the roses, smiling up at him before stepping inside and closing the door.

"What the ever-lovin' hell just happened?" Wyatt asked.

"Zane Tucker happened," Ryder said as they stepped out from behind the bushes.

"Oh yeah." Zane walked up to them, grinning from ear to ear. "What a shock. I came out smellin' like a rose."

They all practically attacked him, but he turned and almost outran them all to the waiting truck.

Adam didn't even try to catch up with him, but walked past the porch, grabbed a red rose, and met them all as the guys piled into the bed of the truck where Bailey was, the whole lot of them laughing like it was some kind of midnight hayride.

God, he loved them all.

He opened the passenger side, grinning at Jane waiting behind the wheel.

And he loved her, too.

"I heard it was a huge success," she said, laughing.

"For Zane," he replied, leaning over to kiss her and offer the rose. "This is for you."

"Aww, thank you. My not-so-secret admirer."

He cupped her face in his hands. "I lied to you once."

She inched back. "Only once?" she teased.

"Only one time. And it wasn't really a lie, but oh man, it was wrong." He stroked her cheek, looking into the dark pools of her eyes.

"What was it?" she asked.

"I told you that you weren't what I was looking for."

"Ah, yes, the big rejection when I tried to get the job."

He almost put his mouth over hers. "You, Jane Anne McAllen, are exactly what I'm looking for."

"Oh, Adam." She curled her hands around his neck. "You're exactly what I've been looking for my whole life. It's like I'm finally home."

"Then you're staying? For sure?" His heart kicked up, knowing that was all he wanted in the world.

"You can't ever get rid of me. In fact, I'm going to help Bailey design the inside of the restaurant, and Hildie told me there are new homes going up not far from here and Garrison Construction wants to hire a designer and—"

"Let's buy one of those houses and live in it together."

She inched back. "Are you serious? Are you sure?"

"How can you even ask that? I love you, Jane. I'm going to love you forever."

She closed her eyes and sighed as if she'd been wrapped in a warm blanket on a cold night. "I love you, too, Adam." She pressed her lips to his, deepening the kiss.

"Hey!" The whole truck shook as someone banged on the back cab window. "I just bet everyone in this truck that you'll be married before summer's over. Did I win or lose, Brother?"

Adam gave a questioning look to Jane, who bit her lip and held his gaze long enough, the question hanging over them.

"Jane?" His heart hammered as he waited for just the slightest nod to confirm what he already knew.

"I want kids," she whispered. "I want to cover them in love and security. I want a home we never leave. And

I only want to change my name one more time."

"Jane Anne Tucker. I love it. I love *you*." He pulled her closer and looked back at Zane. "You won again," he called out. "As always."

His friends howled in wild laughter…just like the old days. And the woman he loved gave him one more kiss…just like the new days that waited in their future.

Adam already knew they'd be the best days of his life.

Don't miss the next book in the

7 Brides for 7 Soldiers
Multi-Author Series

ZANE

by Christie Ridgway

Ex-soldier Zane Tucker is perfectly happy with his single life and his adventure watersports business. A gambler by nature, he figures the odds of finding a woman for forever are a lot longer than finding a woman for right now. And as a man of action and not emotion, he believes a woman with lasting romance on the mind would want someone with less hard muscle and more soft sentiment. But then his dog hurtles toward the new county librarian, yanking Zane into her delicate, pretty presence. Will they both scare her away? And why does that worry him so?

Harper Grace has a bucket list of goals to tick off and is determined to live every moment to the fullest by overcoming her usual shyness. No one will call her too timid and too boring ever again. But then a giant of a man and his equally large dog charge into her life and she can't decide if she wants to take a step back...or step fully into Zane's strong arms. She's been brave enough to change her life, but does she have enough courage to risk her heart?

About the Author

Published since 2003, Roxanne St. Claire is a *New York Times* and *USA Today* bestselling author of fifty romance and suspense novels. She has written several popular series, including The Dogfather, Barefoot Bay, the Guardian Angelinos, and the Bullet Catchers.

In addition to being an eight-time nominee and one-time winner of the prestigious RITA™ Award for the best in romance writing, Roxanne's novels have won the National Readers' Choice Award for best romantic suspense three times, as well as the Maggie, the Daphne du Maurier Award, the HOLT Medallion, Booksellers Best, Book Buyers Best, the Award of Excellence, and many others.

She lives in Florida with her husband, and still attempts to run the lives of her teenage daughter and twenty-something son. She loves dogs, books, chocolate, and wine, especially all at the same time.

www.roxannestclaire.com
www.twitter.com/roxannestclaire
www.facebook.com/roxannestclaire

SIGN UP FOR HER NEWSLETTER AND RECEIVE
A FREE FULL LENGTH NOVEL!
www.roxannestclaire.com/newsletter/